KEELY

A PALMER SISTERS NOVEL: FIVE

KAYT MILLER

CONTENTS

CHAPTER ONE

KEELY

"Fluckity-fluck-fluck."

I must have been too busy singing along to my favorite song to pay attention to my driving, because I just noticed the flashing lights in my rearview mirror. The loud whine of a police siren is barely audible over the music. I wasn't speeding. Was I? Well, maybe I *was* driving just a tad over the limit. My little 2003 Honda Civic is surprisingly zippy. But no worries, I've dodged a ticket or five in the past.

"I'm sure I can get out of this too."

Yeah, I know I'm talking to myself in the car, but it helps to keep me focused on my goal. I know I can do this. I've discovered that all I have to do is flutter my lashes and show my dimple and, bam, I get a warning. Works. Every. Time. Watch and learn, *biatches*.

Looking into my rearview mirror, I watch a man clad in

black police gear stride to the driver side of my car. "Well, hello, Officer Hottie," I whisper to myself.

I lose sight of him for a second, so I roll down my window and spot him in my side mirror. As he approaches, I'm struck by the sheer size of him. He's tall. I can even tell that from my vantage point in my little car. I should add that he's not just tall, he's big. And I mean BIG. His muscles have muscles.

"License, registration, and proof of insurance, please, ma'am."

Ma'am? I'm twenty-five. Ma'am isn't supposed to start until I'm old. Like forty.

"Ma'am. I haven't got all day."

Well, shit. His voice is deep and smooth like sweet, sweet honey. I can imagine the ways he could use that voice.

My attention turns away from thoughts of his sexy tone of voice to the torso in my driver-side window. I scan up his dark uniform, noting how perfectly pressed the thing looks. Then up to the shiny golden badge on his meaty pectoral that reads: *Page, Arizona—To Protect and Serve.*

Mr. Police Officer has dark hair, but I can't see it very well due to his police hat. He's got olive skin and a five o'clock shadow on his chin, which is remarkable since it's only noon. I watch as it tenses like he's gritting his teeth. His lips are stretched thin. Stress. I bet his job is stressful. When my eyes meet his, I only see myself. No, I don't mean that like some romantic sonnet or some shit. I mean I literally see myself in his super-reflective cop aviator sunglasses. My eyes move down to see a very strong nose. There's a little bump on the bridge, which means it's probably been broken before. Not surprising for a cop. My guess is he's been in a tussle or two. My eyes move lower. By the looks of his flaring nostrils, I don't think he's happy.

"Ma'am? Did you hear what I said? License, registration, and proof of insurance. Now."

Damn, he sure is demanding.

"I'm sorry, Officer, but what did I do?" I flutter my eyelashes and ever so subtly push my shoulders back so my chest sticks out just a tiny bit. I say tiny bit because it's all I've got.

With a very heavy sigh, he pulls his glasses off his face, revealing golden brown eyes and long, dark lashes. They're gorgeous. Why do men always get those long lashes? It's so not fair. "Excessive speed and your taillight is out."

Oops. I knew about the taillight, but those are hard to fix. First I'd have to YouTube it, then I'd have to try to buy the replacement bulb, and who knows where you buy one for a car as old as Bluebell. We're talking days of work right there, and let's not forget what a pain it is to undo the plastic cover and the thingamajig to replace the stupid light. Ugh, I'm exhausted just thinking about it.

So, I do what I've gotta do. In as shocked a voice as I can muster, I say, "My taillight is out?"

Ooh, that was good. I even convinced myself I was shocked at the news.

"Yes, ma'am."

Doing my best to look unassuming and cute, I place my palm on my chest like a southern belle fanning herself and flutter my lashes again. I have the urge to say "well fiddle-dee-dee," but instead, in a breathy Marilyn Monroe kind of voice, I say, "Officer, I had no idea."

I watch his eyes roll. That's not a good sign. He's not falling for my cuteness and charm. Strange. It's worked before.

"Ma'am. I'm only going to ask one more time. License, registration, and proof of insurance."

Flustered now, I grab my purse from the seat beside me and

proceed to dump the entire contents of the bag on the seat and floor of the passenger side. "Shit," I mutter.

"Today, ma'am."

I give him a little dirty look but say sweetly, "Oh, sure. Let me find them."

Then I hear his voice rumble even louder as he asks me, "Do you know how fast you were going?"

I turn my head toward him and smile. Bam, there it is, my dimple. "Um, the speed limit?" See, how adorable was that response? I sounded a little dumb but still cute.

"I don't have all day, ma'am."

"Um, okay. Here's my license." I hand him my photo ID and smile again. He's going to love that picture. I took a good one this time, thank goodness. My last license picture made me look like a serial killer. No joke. Ask my sister Violet.

He sighs heavily. Evidently he's got more important things to do. "Now I need your registration and proof of insurance. Sometime today would be nice."

Impatient much?

I'm at a loss for words but I speak anyway. "Right. I'm getting it. Hold your horses."

"Excuse me?"

"I said, hold your horses, geesh."

I abruptly reach over the seat to open my glove box. I must have startled him, because I hear my door being wrenched open.

"Step out of the car, ma'am."

"What?"

"Step. Out. Of. The. Car. Was that clear enough for you?"

"Well, yeah, but you don't have to be a jerk." Forget I ever considered him good-looking. Now he's Officer Not-So-Hot-Anymore. He stands with his left hand on the doorframe and his right hand on his weapon. I quickly unbuckle my seat belt and exit my car. I stand up to my full height and realize that I'm looking right at the shiny badge that's pinned to his front chest pocket. His name, MARTELLI, is forged into the shiny metal shield, but it should say JERKFACE instead. I snort again, aloud. Will I ever learn?

I turn to face my driver-side door, but that's not good enough. "Move to the back of the vehicle, please. Out of the road. Hands on the trunk."

"Yes, Officer Bossypants."

Silence.

"Ma'am, keep your comments to yourself. I don't want to have to take you to the station. Please place your hands on your vehicle and spread your legs."

"I'm getting frisked?" I squeak. "Is that really necessary?"

"Please stop talking, ma'am."

The pat down startles me. I wasn't expecting to get frisked today—or ever, really. I'm a good girl. I'm a kindergarten teacher! Who does this guy think he is? I did nothing wrong! But Officer Meanie says nothing.

He begins the pat down at my sides and his hands move down quickly to my hips and up the inside of my legs. A shiver runs through me that's probably inappropriate under the circumstances. Sue me. I can't help it. The man is cranky *and* hot. A lethal combination.

"You can step back into your car. I'll need your registration and proof of insurance for the ticket."

"Serious? You're going to give me a ticket?"

"Serious. Yes, ma'am. You were traveling forty-five miles per hour in a school zone."

"B-b-but, it's spring break! Schools aren't even in session! I should know." My sputtering, exasperated responses are not helping me at all. I can't believe I've used all my usual charms and I'm still getting a freaking ticket. I mean, I've tried flashing my dimple, fluttering my eyelashes, and I may have stuck my miniscule boobies out so far, I sprained something. And let's not forget the wink.

"Registration, insurance, ma'am. Don't make me ask you again."

I reach into my glove box and grab every paper and booklet in there. I dig through and find what he needs.

He takes my papers and license back to his squad car and I wait. And wait. And I wait some more. How long does it take someone to write a damn speeding ticket? After what seems like hours but was probably more like twenty minutes, Officer A-hole returns with my papers and my lovely parting gift—a $267.40 speeding ticket.

"Two hundred and sixty dollars!?" I squeak. I don't have that kind of money sitting around. I'll have to sell a kidney or something.

"Two sixty-seven." He starts to turn, but stops to add, "And forty cents." Tapping the brim of his hat, he smirks. "Have a good day, ma'am," he says as he walks—no, saunters—back to his police car. Before he slips inside, he turns back to me again. "Slow down and get that taillight fixed."

I'm practically sputtering, but I don't have a reply. I'm in shock. I mean... what a nightmare. My cuteness powers must be dimming. Without those, what's left? Just a boring old *ma'am* of a kindergarten teacher.

CHAPTER TWO

Nick

GOD, I hate traffic duty. I know, I know, we all have to take a turn at traffic duty in our small police department, but it still sucks. Sitting here in my squad car for hours is making my ass numb. Even though I've chosen one of the busiest parts of our small town of Page, it's still boring as hell.

I'm looking around my squad car for something to read when my radar gun begins to beep frantically. Looking up, I see a light blue blur pass my window. Holy hell, the little car was flying. I reach down and flip on my cherries. I grab the gear shift and wrench it into drive and peel out of my spot, checking for oncoming traffic at the same time.

In seconds I've caught up to the little compact car. I reach for my police radio and call in the license plate. It can be dangerous out here, even in a small community like Page. Procedure says I call in the plate to make sure the car isn't stolen—a lesson I learned the hard way.

I've followed the little car for a mile when it occurs to me that the driver has no idea I'm back here. I can barely see the top of a head bobbing about in the car. Listening to the radio, no doubt. I flip on my siren to get their attention and notice the person's head jerk up and peer into the mirror. Instantly, the blinker comes on and the car pulls over to the side of the road. Finally.

Before I open my door, I wait for a few minutes on word from dispatch about the vehicle plate. I notice the driver looking at me, first, in their rearview mirror, then in the side mirror. It's definitely a woman. Or perhaps a girl. Her head barely reaches above the car seat in the tiny Honda. *Is she even old enough to drive?* When I get the all clear, I exit my vehicle and approach the car slowly from the driver side. Sure, I've gotten the go ahead, but I want to take things slowly. It's never good to startle the driver.

I walk confidently to the window and say, "License, registration, and proof of insurance please, ma'am."

After several moments pass, I sense no movement in the vehicle. I bend slightly to peer into the open window. Damn, she's adorable, and she's definitely not a girl. She's probably in her early to mid-twenties, with long blonde hair that shines in the sun. Her eyes are large and startlingly blue-green, and her little turned-up nose rests in the midst of tiny freckles all over her face. I look lower to her lips. Damn, her lips are perfection— plump and tinted a rose-pink hue. She smirks, and a dimple appears on the left side of her face. Fuck, she's got a dimple? I'm a sucker for those.

My eyes slide down her body. She's very compact. Her perky breasts are a little small for my taste, but seeing as they're being intentionally pressed hard against her bra and tank top and practically spilling out, they're more appealing.

She's breathing pretty hard. Is she pissed? Turned on? It

may be a little of both. I've had that reaction from women a time or two. Yeah, I'm a decent-looking guy and fairly popular with the ladies. It doesn't take me much effort to get a woman in my bed, so this little thing is probably no exception. On second thought, she's staring at me like she's in a trance. What's wrong with this chick?

"Ma'am, did you hear what I said? License, registration, and proof of insurance. Now." I sound like a prick, but this is going to take hours if she doesn't pull her cute little head out of her ass.

She reaches for her purse, and fuck if she doesn't dump the entire thing out into her car. *How much shit do you need to carry around with you, ladies?*

"I'm sorry, Officer, but what did I do?" She flutters her eyelashes and ever so subtly pushes her shoulders back further.

With a very heavy sigh, I pull off my sunglasses, "Excessive speed and your taillight is out."

"My taillight is out?" she asks, looking coy. Too coy.

"Yes, ma'am."

"Officer, I had no idea."

I roll my eyes. I can't help it. Why do people think they can get away with this bullshit just to get out of a ticket? No doubt she's gotten away with murder, or a warning in this case. Cops are putty in the hands of some drivers.

I stand impatiently while she digs through the items strewn about her car. "Today, ma'am."

She turns her head and gives me the evil eye. "Oh, sure. Let me find them."

Well, well, well, she's got some fire. She's pissed, and damn, if I could laugh right now, I would. I don't think this little spitfire would appreciate that. I decide to keep things professional, so I ask, "Do you know how fast you were going?"

She turns to me and gives me some of that dimple. "Um, the speed limit?"

She's trying to play the dumb blonde card again. It's not going to work. "I don't have all day, ma'am."

"Um, okay. Here's my license." She hands me her ID and gives me a broad smile. Her teeth are perfect. I peer down at her license and read her name. Keely May Palmer. She looks like a Keely May. Her address is listed as 1627 Willington Court, Apartment 6B, Page. So, she lives here in town. I'd like to ask her how long she's lived here, but it's best if I don't ask her personal questions. It's been hard enough getting her registration and proof of insurance.

I sigh. "Now I need your registration and proof of insurance. Sometime today would be nice."

She scoffs as she says, "Right. I'm getting it. Hold your horses."

"Excuse me?" Is she becoming belligerent with an officer of the law?

"I said, hold your horses, geesh."

It's then that she abruptly reaches over across the passenger seat. I have no idea what she's doing, but any action that happens that quickly can be dangerous. I grab her door handle, yank it open, and shout, "Step out of the car, ma'am.

"What?" she says, looking completely confused.

That's when I succinctly say, "Step. Out. Of. The. Car. Was that clear enough for you?"

"Well, yeah, but you don't have to be a jerk."

Oh, she did not just say that. I stand, holding her door open with my left hand while I reach down and rest my right hand on my gun. I've learned that you can't trust anyone when you're out on the mean streets. Even tiny little women can be dangerous.

Finally, she unbuckles her seat belt and exits the car. She

stands directly in front of me, and that's when it hits me just how small she is. She can't be more than five feet tall. The top of her head barely reaches my chest. As I check her out now, I can tell that she is indeed a compact woman, but what I didn't notice from her seated position in her car were her soft curves. The woman is built like a goddess.

"Turn around and face the car, ma'am."

"Yes, Officer Bossypants."

Jesus, she's got a smart mouth. I decide to bite my lip. "Ma'am, keep your comments to yourself. I don't want to take you to the station. Please place your hands on your vehicle and spread your legs."

She turns to face my driver side door, but this can't happen here. She needs to move. She's too close to the road. "Move to the back of the vehicle, please. Out of the road. Hands on the trunk."

"I'm getting frisked?" she shouts. "Is that really necessary?"

"Please stop talking ma'am." Seriously, stop talking. I really don't want to arrest her.

As I start the patting at her sides and move down past her breasts, I feel my dick twitch. Certainly not the most professional reaction to a pat-down I've ever had. I stop for just a second to regroup, then continue moving my hands down. I'm sure she's not concealing anything, but I need to follow through here. My hands shift further down onto her curvy hips to her thighs, and then downward to her slim ankles. I continue up the inside of her legs like my training has taught me. Even though she's wearing shorts—tiny shorts—I still have to move through the standard process of a frisk. It's departmental policy. As my fingers slide up her legs, I quickly finish the frisk and step back standing abruptly. Clearing my throat, I say, "You can step back into your car. I'll need your registration and proof of insurance for the ticket."

"Serious? You're going to give me a ticket?"

"Serious," I deadpan. "Yes, ma'am. You were traveling forty-five miles per hour in a school zone."

"B-b-but, it's spring break! Schools aren't even in session! I should know." She's getting pretty flustered now.

"Registration, insurance, ma'am. Don't make me ask you again." She reaches into the glove compartment and grabs every single piece of paper and booklet in there, and there's a bunch of papers and booklets. It seems impossible that it all fit in there.

Finally, she hands me her insurance card and registration. I've aged twenty years since this whole thing started. I grab her papers and head back to the squad car to do a records check on this girl. It's time to learn a little more about Miss Keely May Palmer. Or is it Mrs.?

I hope not.

After checking her out, I see a slew of warnings issued to *Miss* Keely Palmer. It's time someone had the balls to fine her. I write out her ticket. I leave off the taillight this time since she obviously didn't have time to fix that before now. Besides, it's a steep penalty for speeding in a school zone, but it's time for her to pay a fine, and hopefully she'll drive a little slower and safer in the future.

After sending in Keely Palmer's citation information to dispatch, I pull back out onto the road to make another sweep of my route. Checking the clock on the dash, I make a mental note that I've only got an hour left in a shift that feels a week long. Pulling up to a stop sign and preparing to turn onto Lincoln Street, I flip on my turn signal just as a light blue blur passes through the intersection in front of me. My speed sensor starts to beep loudly. I blink at the old Honda speeding, literally, westbound on a main thoroughfare.

You've got to be shitting me.

CHAPTER THREE

KEELY

"WHAT ARE YOU DOING?" My oldest sister Lainie looks at me, perplexed.

"I'm just making some notes to prepare."

"Prepare? For what?"

"My court battle." I shrug.

Lainie's mouth drops open, then shuts quickly. "Court battle?"

I roll my eyes and sigh. I'm doing my best to move this little convo along. "My appeal."

"Appeal?"

"Yeah."

"For what?"

"Oh, just a speeding ticket." Or two.

She looks at the rectangular piece of paper sitting on the table in front of me and blinks. "Not a warning this time?"

"No," I grumble. "But nothing to worry about, sis."

"Uh-huh."

I look over at my sister and see she's got her hands on her hips. I know that stance. I counter her stance with a hand placed over my heart and up the ante with a pathetic look on my face. "Lainie, I'm innocent."

"Uh-huh. So you're appealing the ticket?"

Tickets. But who's counting? "Yep." I nod. "It was entrapment." Sure, I know he didn't actually *entrap* me. Oh, hell, why does the thought of one Officer Nick Martelli entrapping me sound so delicious? *No, Keely! Focus.* My court date is right around the corner. I need to prepare.

"Right." Lainie stares at me, then shouts, "Wait! You didn't get a ticket in Keeton's car, did you?

Lainie has somehow gotten hold of a car worth about fifty thousand bucks. A car belonging to some biker dude she's got the hots for. I've been able to drive it once, since my car is now inexplicably being worked on at the biker dude's shop. There was nothing wrong with Bluebell. (Lainie calls her Bessie, but that's just wrong.) She's rock solid.

"Not yet." I wink. "But, there's still time."

Lainie mutters, "You won't have time. Our car is going to be done soon."

"Well, that's a damn shame, sis. That's a sweet-ass ride." At least if I rode around in *that* car, Mr. Hot Cop wouldn't know it was me. But what kind of fun would that be?

CHAPTER FOUR

KEELY

IT'S BEEN two weeks since I submitted my request to appeal the ticket, and today, I finally got notification of my court date. April 1 at 1:00 p.m. Even though it's weeks away, a chill of nerves rushes through my body. Perhaps it's nerves due to the fact I've never been to court before, or it could be because I'll get to see one Officer Nick "Sexy Boots" Martelli? Probably the latter. Why would I be excited to see him? He's arrogant. And bossy. *Oh, so very bossy.*

Stop, Keely! I've got to stop thinking about him. I need to focus on this class—a class I'm taking for my teacher license renewal. It's kind of a pain, but it's just part of being an educator. The good thing is, I'm not alone. I'm taking a life drawing class with my trusty teacher sidekicks: Michael, my work husband. He's gay so he'd never agree to marry me in real life, but he can still be my work husband. He's a kindergarten teacher too. His room is right next to mine, which is awesome because we co-teach a lot and being neighbors makes it super handy.

Then there's Sally, Julia, and Kimberly. They're all first grade teachers who get our little hellions the year after we do. Don't get me wrong; I say hellion in the best possible way. I love my little people. Like a lot. A lot, a lot. Every year I cry for a week when my babies move up to the next grade.

"So, who the hell was the fucking genius who thought we should take an art class?" Sometimes Michael can be such a bitch.

"Me, asshole. I like art." I need to keep going, badger him. He'll relent if I keep right on going. "Like it would do you harm to learn some art. Your kiddos will *love* to do some art. Visual learners? Ever heard of those. Geesh." I sigh. "And another thing—"

"Fine!" he shouts. "Damn, woman. You win. Uncle. I'll do whatever you say if it means you'll stop talking."

See? Nobody messes with a badger.

"Since you two lovebirds are done arguing, Keely, can you please tell us what we're doing here?"

"It's life drawing." Duh. "We're going to draw things that are alive." I assume.

"You have no idea what we're doing. Do you?"

Grrrr. Michael.

"Shh, the teacher is ready to start." A good save if I do say so myself, because no, I have no idea what we're doing in this class.

The teacher, Ms. Priscilla Price, or Ms. P as I used to call her in elementary school, is older. I'd say midsixties if I had to guess, and she's a wonderful teacher. She was my art teacher all through elementary school. I think she was my sisters' too. Maybe not Lainie's. I shrug internally. One thing about Ms. P? She's the sweetest lady in the world until you piss her off. Then, damn, you'd wish you were anywhere else. She doesn't put up with any bullshit, which I can appreciate.

"Hello, boys and girls," she says in a sweet voice. God, I love her. "Tonight is your first night in life drawing, so we're going to start off with a bang."

Michael snorts because he's got a filthy mind like that.

Truth? I snorted too.

"We have a special guest model tonight. He's doing us a great favor by taking time out of his busy schedule to pose for you." Ms. Priscilla raises her hand, motioning toward a side door. "Please welcome my nephew, Nicholas."

Like it's choreographed, we all turn toward the door as it slowly opens. I see a foot emerge first. It's bare, and from here I can see dark hair on the top of the foot. I scrunch up my nose at that. I'm not sure how I feel about hairy feet. I mean, if the feet are hairy, it probably means other unsightly things are hairy. I shiver, thinking of things like a hairy back. The door opens a few more inches, and a leg covered in a white robe begins to emerge. My eyes move up as the door opens further, revealing more of him. Finally, the door pushes open the rest of the way and he's there, Nicholas.

Ms. Priscilla's nephew and the cop I'm fighting in court are one and the same—Nick Martelli.

He comes out in a robe. Only a robe. There are gasps and mutters all around the room. I swear I hear Michael moan. I'm not surprised the rest of the class is doing the same, because Nick Martelli is *gorgeous*. Even in a robe. A small robe that is pulling away from his chest. A chest covered in tufts of dark hair. It's secured tightly with a matching belt around his trim waist. The realization hits. Nick Martelli is the model in life drawing? Is he going to be naked? Holy shit. *Please say yes.*

"Welcome, Nicholas."

"Thank you, Aunt P," Nick says in that sexy, honeyed voice.

If he weren't so tanned, I'd guess he was blushing. That's kinda cute.

"Nicholas is a wonderful boy," Ms. P says, beaming.

I scowl, remembering he's not so wonderful when he's giving tickets. When I look up, he's staring; his expression matches mine. He doesn't look happy.

What? What'd I do? He's the one doling out stupid tickets.

Ms. Priscilla keeps right on going. "He just moved to town recently, and I'm so glad he did. Nicholas does such good works for our community every day. Why, even today he's volunteering so I don't have to spend my own money on a model. Isn't he wonderful?"

Ah, that's why I've never seen him before. He just moved to town.

There's a collective sigh and a hissing "yes" heard around the room. Yeah, Nick Martelli is definitely giving back. I snicker again. I can't help it, I'm hilarious.

"Please turn to your first sheet of paper in your drawing pad. I'd like for you to use conté crayon for this." Ms. Priscilla says, holding up a black stick for us all to see. Looking through my drawing supplies, I find what I need.

"You won't be able to erase."

The entire room groans.

"Now, now. It's fine. We're going to do some gesture drawings to warm you up. No erasing when we're warming up." Ms. P. begins by asking Nick to remove his robe. I swear, I hear every single person hold their breath the minute he reaches for the tie that's holding the flimsy terry cloth in place. Me included. Right at the moment of truth, Ms. P stops him, saying, "Nicholas, we're going to do some quick poses. Thirty seconds apiece. Do you remember what I told you?"

"Yes, Aunt Priscilla."

Another "Aw" sounds around the room. A woman behind me declares, "What a nice boy."

It makes me giggle again. It also gets me another glare from Mr. Schmexy.

All eyes turn to Nick as he reaches for the tie around the robe again. In slow-motion like those running scenes in *Baywatch*, Officer Nick Martelli slowly, so fucking slowly, pulls open the robe. The room gasps loudly this time.

"Holy shit. I love this class!" shouts Michael, loud enough for everyone to hear.

I lose it. As do Sally, Kimberly, and Julia.

When I get myself under control, I know I need to pay attention to class, but I'm afraid to look at him.

"I think I just came a little," whispers Julia, and that's all it takes to start us laughing again.

Finally, I look up. Sadly, he's not naked. But what he's wearing is almost... *almost* as good. He's wearing black boxer briefs that are snug all over—they hug *everything*.

"Look how strategically he places his junk." Michael's staring at Nick's crotch.

"You'd know," mutters Sally.

"I sure would. Or should I say wood, w-o-o-d."

I snort.

"He'd have to. Look at the size of him." Kimberly pauses. "It. The size of *it*."

I cackle, I can't help it. "I love you guys."

When Nick turns to face his aunt, I get a glimpse of his firm ass. The class of eighteen women and one man sits in stunned silence as Ms. Priscilla gets him situated.

"So, how do you want me?" he asks his aunt, and the crowd moans simultaneously.

"I'd take him anywhere he wants," says a voice behind me. I crane my neck to see a woman who has to be in her eighties.

I nod to her and wink. She's got a good eye.

The first pose has Nick standing with his hands at his narrow waist, his legs spread. I pick up my crayon and begin to draw just like Ms. P showed us. The next pose has one of Nick's feet placed onto a chair and his arms outstretched. It's a good look for him. You get to see all of the muscles in his arms that way.

After twenty minutes of those quick sketches, Ms. P. switches things up. She poses him on a chaise lounge with one foot on the ground and the other foot on the chair, his knee bent. One of his hands is behind his head, the other rests on the raised knee. It's a sexy pose.

Fortunately, or unfortunately, depending on how you see it, he's now facing us. Me, precisely. His eyes are on me, and it's unnerving the way they move from my face down to my chest. I'm wearing a fairly low-cut tank top today. I suppose you could say I'm showing some skin. I didn't mean to, it's just I'm with my friends and the tank is old and comfy. Perfect for an art class. When our eyes meet, I see the corner of his mouth twitch up just slightly. Then, I swear, he winks. At me. Okay, I could be wrong. I could have imagined it. It could have been more of a twitch. Or he could be winking at the gran behind me. Okay, call it wishful thinking. But it really seemed like the wink, twitch, whatever, was directed at me.

"Um, Ms. Priscilla," says Michael, with his hand raised. Kindergarten teacher move, for sure.

"Yes? Uh?"

"Michael," he says, placing his hand on his chest. Then he turns to look squarely at Nick. "Michael Brooks. 928-432-1039." Then he winks.

One of my girls coughs; another one giggles.

Damn, he's good.

"Did you have a question, Michael?" Ms. Priscilla smiles at Michael sweetly.

Brown-noser.

"Oh, right. Are we supposed to use the crayon thing again?"

"No, my dear. Please switch to your pencils. You may erase as needed. Nicholas will sit in this pose for much longer. I won't give you any instruction for this first drawing. I'd like to see where you are in terms of skill level so I know who needs the most help."

I place my hand over my mouth and fake cough, "Michael."

"Hey!" He sounds affronted. "Fuck you, bitch." Then he laughs. "True, though."

As soon as Ms. Priscilla asks us to start, I pick up my pencil but stop. "I have no idea where to start," I grumble.

"Start at the crotch and move up. That's what I'm doing," Michael says quietly.

We all giggle uncontrollably at that. I stare at Michael's paper as he ever so slowly begins to draw Nick's, uh, bulge. Okay. Fine. He starts at his dick. Happy?

When the thirty minutes are up, Ms. P lets Nick stand and stretch. I watch, because why wouldn't I? After he's got his robe back on, I stand as well. From the corner of my eye, I see him begin to walk around the room, looking at everyone's drawings. When he sees Julia's, he stops. It's no wonder; hers is amazing. I had no idea the little traitor could draw.

I hear him tell her how good her drawing is and that he may have to buy it. A tinge of jealousy overtakes me, but I quickly push it down. It's not about the drawing, but I shouldn't worry; she's married. No need to feel competitive. Right?

Next, he moves to Michael's and smiles but says nothing. When he looks at mine, he laughs. "Miss Palmer?"

What the hell? He's laughing at mine? I jam my hands on my hips and give him my sassiest look. "Yeah?" I don't know what else to say to him when he's standing this close and wearing only a robe. *Get it together, Keels.* Remember. First off, he's a cop. Not only that but he's a cop that gave me three tickets in less than thirty minutes.

"So, art isn't your thing?" he asks smugly.

I harrumph. I can't draw. I'm terrible. But that's not my issue. "I just can't focus. I didn't know where to start."

Michael interjects, "I told her to start at your crotch and move up. That's what I did!" He smiles. Michael's piece seems to be out of proportion. There was a lot of work done in the crotch area and midsection, but the head was sort of... well, there wasn't one.

I snicker at his, which seems to amuse Nick too. Nick looks at me and says, "I think your friend has the right idea. I would always recommend starting at the crotch and working up." He winks.

What the ever-loving fuck? I blush. I can't help it, and it sucks because I rarely blush.

Nick attempts to whisper in my ear, but he's not good at it. My friends all hear him say, "You're cute when you blush."

I hate when people call me cute. But I hate ma'am worse, so I guess I'll take it.

I'm sort of shocked by his words. I'm speechless, which doesn't happen very often. Or never. Yeah, I'll go with never.

"She doesn't like to be called cute," says Kimberly.

"Why not? She *is* cute. She's got freckles, big doe eyes, and she's even got a dimple. She's adorable."

I would swear that he's fucking with me. This isn't the same asshole who pulled me over *twice* and wrote tickets *both times*! No, this guy is actually sort of nice.

I'm about to rebut when Ms. P claps her hands. "Boys and girls? Let's get started. Please turn to a clean page."

Nick quickly moves back to the center of the room as his

aunt has him pose in a new position. This time he's standing. One hand is on the back of the lounge chair, while the other is on his hip. His left leg is bent slightly.

"Boys and girls?" snickers Michael. "What are we? Kindergartners?"

I glare at him. Ms. P is awesome. "She's used to teaching little kids. Deal with it, you punk-ass..." I pause, trying to come up with something clever to end that statement. "...punk."

"Oooh, good one," Michael deadpans. "I am rubber, you are glue. Anything you say bounces off me and sticks to you!"

I roll my eyes but inwardly laugh. I love Michael. He's always fun.

"This pose, ladies and gents..."

Oops. Better listen.

"...is something we artists call contrapposto. The leg is bent, and the hip is out. Please begin when you're ready."

It's a good pose. I get to see most of his ass and his back. He's got a great back. It's really ripped with muscles bulging out. It's too bad he's the damn enemy. Cops. *I hate cops*. I can't forget that. I need to keep my head straight about this guy. I refuse to let him flirt and distract me from my end goal—bringing him down.

CHAPTER FIVE

Nick

WHAT THE HELL are you doing, Nick?

The last thing I need is to get entangled with someone like Keely Palmer. Sure, she's cute and sexy and curvy but she's the last thing I need right now. I moved here two months ago for a fresh start. A new beginning after the shit I dealt with in Phoenix. I chose Page for two reasons. One, my aunt lives here. She's always been my rock, my voice of reason since my mom passed, because my dad was—is—a self-centered prick. Reason two is because Page, Arizona, is a small town. The pace is slow and there's been no gun violence here in years. Slow and safe is what I need right now. That's not to say I won't feel like heading back to a major city someday, but not now. No, now I need this. I need the time to deal with my issues, namely guilt.

After class ends, I hang out and wait for Aunt Priscilla. Honest to God, the woman is my saving grace. I've always adored her, even with her rather eccentric way of life and thinking. In the past there've been times I questioned her sanity. Like the time she decided she wanted to become a psychic; it was her *calling* from her earth goddess. See what I mean? No matter, the woman has the heart of a saint, so that's pretty close to a goddess in my book. She was there for me when my ma passed away. She was there when my dad flaked out on me and just up and left a week after her funeral. I was eighteen, a man already, but it still stung. I haven't heard a word from him since.

I haven't missed him. I graduated high school, then enlisted in the army without him; I attended the police academy and graduated without him, and I nearly lost my partner on the force during a routine traffic stop without him. *Fuck him.*

I shake away the negative thoughts the minute Aunt P steps out from the back room.

"Ready, Nicholas?"

"Ready." I smile and let her slide her arm through mine. "Do you want to get a bite to eat before I take you home?"

"Oh, you're the sweetest. But I've got soup in my slow cooker and fresh dinner rolls. I was hoping you'd have a bite to eat with me."

Hell, yeah! Aunt P cooks like a boss. "I'd love to. Thanks."

SITTING in Aunt Priscilla's kitchen, I'm about to take a big spoonful of soup when she says, "She's cute, isn't she?"

My spoon stops in midair. My mouth is wide open, anticipating the first taste. *She knows.* The little devil knows. *Play dumb, Nick. Just play dumb.* "She?"

My aunt chuckles. "You always liked to play dumb with me." In a teasing tone, she says, "No, Aunt P. I didn't eat the last cookie." She looks at me with her all-knowing eyes. "No, Aunt P, I didn't throw the baseball through the window."

"I didn't do that. It was Kenny." The next-door neighbor. "He ran off before you could catch him."

"Uh-huh. So?"

With a sigh, I set the spoon down. I can never get anything past this woman. "It *was* Kenny, and her name is—"

"Keely Palmer. I've known her since she was little."

"She was your student?"

"She and her sisters." Aunt P sighs. "I also knew her mother before she passed, and I know her father."

"You did? You do?"

"Of course. I've lived here nearly all my life."

Aunt P was born in Italy, but her parents immigrated here when she was a baby.

"And?"

"And, her mother, God rest her, was charming and vivacious."

Her mother died? Like mine. "How?"

"Cancer. I'm not sure which kind." Aunt P shakes her head. "She was a lovely and kind woman. A redhead, as I recall. It was sad those girls lost their mother at such young ages."

"That is sad." At least I was an adult when I lost mine. I had her for eighteen years.

"It is." Using the ladle, she serves herself a half bowl of chicken noodle soup. Entirely handmade. Even the noodles.

I spoon my first bite into my mouth and moan. "Mm, good."

"I'm glad you like it." She takes a sip of hers and smiles. "Yep. I'm a good cook."

I chuckle between spoonfuls of noodles. "You are."

"She's got a twin."

"Who?"

"Keely."

"There's two of them running around?" I'd laugh, but the thought of two of them makes me shudder.

"They look nothing alike. Violet is tall, and her hair is like their mother's. But by the way Keely always giggled in class, I think she got some of her mother's personality."

Okay, good to know. I nod but keep eating.

"One of her other sisters owns the bakery."

"Sadie Cakes?" That place is delicious. "Good stuff."

"Indeed."

"Lainie, the oldest, I believe, just got out of a terrible marriage."

"Terrible? How so?"

"Loveless. You could see it all over her face. Poor girl."

"Who was she married to?"

"Lewis Bottoms."

"The banker?" I met him at a city council meeting the first week on the job, and I'd bet my badge he's gay. Now, before you think I'm judging, I'm not. I couldn't care less. It's just that I recall him checking me out and standing just a little too close to me. I can see why the marriage may not have worked out.

"And then there's Agatha. She works at the big shoe company in town."

The list keeps growing. "How many sisters does she have?"

"Five girls. Five little girls without their mama. But Rob did an amazing job. He's a good man."

I nod as I take the last bite from my bowl.

"Have another. I'll put some into a container for your lunch tomorrow."

I should tell her not to bother, but I don't take the time to cook for myself these days and I'm pretty damn sick of ham sandwiches. "Thanks, Aunt P."

Patting my cheek, she smiles. "You're welcome, sweetheart."

I take a drink of my milk just as she adds, "If you play your cards right, you could have that little Keely Palmer making your lunch."

I nearly spit out the milk. Coughing, I say, "Aunt P, I don't need a woman to make my meals." Besides, I'm surprised by how outdated that sounded. "These days women aren't required to cook." I chuckle because I know what's coming. Aunt P is a feminist.

"Now, you know I didn't mean it like that. Of course you can make your own soup, Nicholas Bernard Martelli."

Oh, shit. She broke out the middle name. The one that sounds like something you'd name your dog. *Thanks, Dad.*

"And another thing. All I meant was you could sure use someone to take care of you and vice versa. Sheesh."

Aunt P doesn't have someone in her life to take care of her. Well, she didn't until I moved here. I blink at my dearest relative. She looks a little sad. Maybe that's why she thinks I need someone. "I hear you, A.P., but Keely Palmer is a spitfire. Too much for me to—"

"Bullshit."

What?! I cough and laugh at the same time. Aunt Priscilla doesn't ordinarily cuss so it's surprising hearing that kind of language from her. "Excuse me?" I chuckle some more.

"You heard me. Besides, you could use a little fire in your life, son."

Standing up from the table, I wrap my arm around her. "Why would I need another spitfire? I've got you."

I laugh as I take my dishes to the kitchen sink.

"That's funny stuff, Nicholas. Just listen to your aunt. I know things."

She sure does. Sometimes it's uncanny what she knows.

I PULL into the driveway of my three-bedroom house. I bought it after only seeing the pictures online. Well, Captain Morgan checked it out for me since I couldn't get up here to house hunt before I started working. I was lucky; it turned out to be a very solid house in a great neighborhood. The only thing it needed, and still needs, is some updates and decorating. It's pretty sparse at the moment, but I'll get to that. Someday.

The house is dark and quiet. Sitting in my SUV, I think about what Aunt Priscilla said. She's right about one thing; I could use a little fire in my life. Hell, I could use just about anything interesting in my life. The newness of my change of jobs and relocation has worn off. I've got a routine now. Too much of one, to be honest. I wanted low-key; I got low-key. I wanted low stress; I got no stress. I wanted to work alone after what happened to my partner, Melissa. I no longer want the worry that accompanies a partner on the force.

Poor Melissa.

It was my fault, after all. The guilt is overwhelming at times, but at least she survived. Scarred for life, literally, but she survived. At least I did that for her; I got her help fast enough.

"Fuck." I run my palms over my face and sigh.

Pushing open the door of my car, I step out onto my driveway and make my way inside. Alone. Just like I want it.

CHAPTER SIX

KEELY

"OKAY, LITTLE BEANS." That's what I call my students. *Little beans.* Why? Because. Well, it's cute. I don't know why I started doing that, but I did, and it fits. There are a gazillion different kinds of beans out there, just like there are different kinds of people. Kindergartners are no exception.

"We're going to talk about *buuuuugs.*" I emphasis the word bugs to get a rise out them. About half of my little beans like bugs; the others think they are "blechy." Their word, not mine.

I've got all sixteen of my beans on the carpet in the reading nook with their legs in criss-cross applesauce. It's imperative to get them sitting like this. It helps keep the fidgety and squirmy ones in place for longer. As it is, I've only got about eight minutes before they'll need to get up and do something else.

"Let me read you some names of bugs. Funny names. You ready?" I've created an art project for this lesson within a larger unit about insects. See? I'm thinking about my visual learners. Thank you, Ms. P.

"Yessss!" they say in unison. Well, almost. Mason always has to shout louder and longer than everyone else, so his is more like "Yesssssssssssssss."

"Mason," I say like a boss. I hold my finger over my lips, giving him the universal *shhh* sign. He does so, reluctantly.

"Here we go." I pause to get them excited. "Rhinoceros Beetle."

The kids all giggle. Nothing sounds sweeter than the laughter of my precious babes.

"Woolly Bear Caterpillar." I smile as the kids laugh. "Wolf Spider," I say with a really growly voice. I play with my voice for each of the bug names, doing my best to sound like the creature I'm talking about. Using my voice to create characters helps make everything more engaging for the kids. "Sheep Moth," I say with a *baaaah* in my voice. Because I can't imitate a buffalo, I hop up and down when I say, "Buffalo Treehopper."

I set my list in my lap, because I want to get them involved. "Do you know any bug names?"

They all begin to shout at once. Placing my finger over my lips, I wait until they calm down. "Little beans. Remember. I need to see hands raised."

One by one, they name all the bugs they know. The list includes insects we all know like ladybugs, butterflies, crickets, and—yuk—cockroaches. I'm about to continue reading my list when one little hand goes up in the back. "Yes, Augustus."

"Um." He hesitates. "Olivia has bugs."

Oh, no! Olivia has been gone for several days now because she, in fact, does have bugs. *Lice.* Lots of kids get lice, especially when they're surrounded by lots of other kiddos. I'm superstitious, so that means I need to knock on some wood. You know, so I don't get lice. I've been lucky so far. I've avoided those gross little fuckers. Looking around for something made of wood, I decide to use the arm of my chair. I knock, then quickly return to my list, only nodding and smiling at Augustus. Reading off the rest of my list, I ask the kids to return to their desks.

"Today we're going to do an art project related to our bug unit. That means you get to use your imagination!" I clap, because I want to encourage them to always be creative. "Plus, you get to use the art supplies I've placed in the middle of your tables."

They all cheer. "You get to be as imaginative, weird, and silly as you want. So here's how it works. I'm going to tell you a bug name that is super-duper-silly sounding. I have never seen this bug, but it's a real one. I want you to draw me a picture of what you think this bug would look like." I've placed paper and bins filled with crayons, water soluble markers, and pencils on their tables. I look out at them in their tiny chairs and tiny tables. God, they're adorable. "Ready?"

"Ready, Miss Palmer!" several shout.

"Here it is." I pause for dramatic effect. It's working. I swear some of them are holding their breath. I want to giggle but I can't. I will when I tell Michael how this worked out. "Ant Lion," I roar loudly.

My kids erupt in laughter, and it gives me happy shivers. I love my job.

"SO, how'd the art lesson go?" Michael asks me, biting into some fresh sushi.

Where the hell did he get fresh sushi?

"Good." I smile at Michael as we quickly eat our lunch. "There were some pretty funny drawings." And by funny, I mean creative. "I'll show you before we go to the in-service."

Michael grumbles. "I hate in-service days."

We have them every Wednesday after the kids get out early. "Me too." And today's is one I've been dreading. Safety training. In our case, we're getting self-defense training in case there's an active shooter in the building. It's so fucking sad that we have to do this.

CHAPTER SEVEN

Nick

I'M STANDING behind my captain as he talks to the auditorium filled with teachers, staff, and administrators from Page CSD. Scanning the crowd earlier, I spotted her sitting with the same group from the art class. I'm doing my best to ignore her, but I can't help it. She's constantly moving, whispering to her friends, and giggling. It pisses me off, to be honest. This is important training. Trust me. I've been a first responder to many shootings, several considered "mass" shootings, in my career. Those scenes were like war zones.

Just as Captain Morgan begins to tell them about our breakout sessions, I see movement to my left. It's her. Keely Palmer, leaning forward to talk to someone in front of her, using her hands as she talks. *She's not even listening.* I grit my teeth. The girl needs a reality check. Or a spanking. *Shit, no, Nick. Don't go there.*

"So, let's break you up into two groups," says the captain. "If you're on the left side of the room, you'll meet in the cafeteria to run through active killer drills."

That's what we call them now: Active killers. Because that's what those motherfuckers are. Murderers.

"If you're on the right, you're going to stay in here for some basic self-defense instruction. Any questions?"

I look over at her, half expecting her to ask some asinine question because she hasn't been listening.

I step out into the cafeteria and wait for my group to arrive. As they enter, I ask them all to take a face mask. There are about fifty people in my session. A good number for running the drills I've got planned today. Once they've all got masks, I ask them to gather around me and then I introduce myself.

"Hello, I'm Nick Martelli. I'm an ex-Army Ranger, and before coming to Page, I was on the Phoenix police force." I hesitate, expecting questions. When I don't hear any, I continue. "Unfortunately, I've been a first responder to many shootings, including several mass shootings. The information I'm about to give you could save your life."

The audience is silent. I see Keely's male companion in the back. It's hard to miss him; he's taller than I am by several inches. I assume she's near him, so I'm rather surprised they aren't chatting and laughing.

"We're going to run three drills today. We'll use the three classrooms adjacent to the cafeteria. Each has a different setup. One has a window looking in from the hallway, one has an exit that leads outside, and another has only a door and no windows. You'll split up into three groups. I'd like you to experience each drill from a different room. Make sense?"

The group nods.

"Great. Now, who wants to be the shooter?"

I look around the room and watch as faces drain of color and mouths drop open. "I need a shooter for this first demonstration."

Finally, a hand in the front of the room goes up. "I'll do it." I recognize her. She's the elementary school principal. I believe her name is Pam.

"Our shooter will be using this." I hold up an air pistol. "It shoots plastic BBs. The masks will protect your faces, but if you're shot, you'll feel it. If you would like to opt out of the drill, please let me know as soon as I'm finished explaining it."

I see a few nods, but the group is quiet.

Turning to Pam, I ask, "Can you step out of the room for now?" To make this as authentic as possible, I don't want her to know what the plan is.

"Sure."

I wait until she's out of the cafeteria and then turn and say to the group, "You'll choose a room and sit as if you're in a regular classroom. At some point, I'll sound this airhorn." I raise it up and press the button, startling most of the group. Some even cover their ears. "That will alert you to gunshots."

I look around, expecting what, I'm not sure. "For this first drill, the only thing you can do is hide beneath your desk."

I see a small hand raise in the back. I can't see who it belongs to.

"Can we use our desks as cover?"

It sounds a lot like Keely, but I can't be sure.

"Yes. You can pull the desk down in front of you. No running or locking the doors."

"Our classroom doors don't lock from the inside," says a woman in the front.

I know. I checked out each room and the area around the school to give myself the lay of the land. Part of the training required that I do a preliminary assessment of the school's readiness for something like this. From that assessment of Page

Elementary, I have recommended some changes, including addressing the issues with classroom doors opening out instead of in and the fact that they've got no inside locks. "I'm aware."

"Any other questions?" When I hear none, I tell them all to take their places.

As they split up into the three rooms, I seek out my shooter. I tell her how this will work. I give her the air pistol.

"I'm really shooting them?" She blanches.

"You are. Avoid their heads. You've only got about three to seven minutes, so keep that in mind as you're moving from room to room." Three to seven minutes is about the amount of time a shooter has before they either flee the scene, get taken out by law enforcement, or end their own lives.

"This is so sick."

Patting her shoulder, I nod. "It is, but it's necessary."

As soon as everyone is in place, I sound the horn and watch as the principal steps into each room, shooting anyone she can see.

When I call everyone back, I ask for a show of hands of the number of people who were shot. I count fifteen hands. One of them was Keely, and for some inexplicable reason, that bothers me more than it should.

It's just a drill.

I continue. "Statistically, it's typical for about a quarter of people involved to be shot. Shooters generally have terrible aim, since they likely purchased a weapon in the six months to several weeks prior to an event and haven't had extensive training with the weapon."

I ask for questions and for reactions. I'm not surprised to hear that many of them felt breathless during the ordeal. Some even thought their hearts were going to explode from fear.

"Your feelings are all normal." I look around for more questions. "Okay, I need another shooter."

This time, Keely raises her hand. I ask her to leave the room so I can give the group instructions. I advise them to go to a different room and tell them they can barricade themselves in the room or attempt to escape.

Once everyone is in place, I walk to Keely, who's standing just outside the cafeteria. Her face is pale.

"You okay?"

"No." She looks up at me, and I see real fear in her eyes. "This is too real."

Placing my hand on her shoulder, I feel something. What, I'm not sure. "I know. But if this empowers you, gives you the skills to save yourself...."

"Myself?" she squeaks. "I don't care about me. It's my little beans I'm worried about."

"Little beans?"

"My kiddos. My classroom. They're just b-babies." Her eyes begin to water, and I do what anyone would do. I wrap her up in my arms.

"I know. Learning this will help you. You should always do what you can to save yourself first."

"No," she whispers. "Why?"

"So *you*, Keely Palmer"—I squeeze her shoulder to reassure her—"can save *them*."

CHAPTER EIGHT

I CAN'T EXPLAIN how I'm feeling right now, because I have no clue what those feelings are. I know I'm confused. He makes it hard to keep my promise. I know I'm being held by a cop. Sure, he's not just any cop, but he's a cop nonetheless. A cop that's here to help us. This particular cop is reassuring me, and it feels good. Too good. He seems bigger than I remember, and his chest is just as hard as it looks. In a good way. His big arms are wrapped around me. My cheek is against his chest, and goddamn— he smells good. Like a forest. Okay. A forest is not the best word to describe his scent, but it's woodsy and nice. I wonder if he's an outdoorsman.

"Do you camp?"

Shit. I actually asked that. Aloud.

"Uh." He stops rubbing my back, and it sucks. "Sometimes? Why?"

"No reason." I pull back from him, and it saddens me. "I'm ready."

"You sure?"

No. I can't believe I volunteered to be the shooter. "Yes."

He shows me how to fire the pistol, and when I'm in the right mindset, I nod, letting him know he can sound the horn. I run down the hallway to the first room, the one with the window. I can see movement in the room, but when I attempt to open the door outward, something is stopping it. I lean in to see if I can get a shot, but I can't. I tug on the door one more time but it's not budging. I look through the window again and see why. It's because someone has wrapped a belt over the knob and has it attached to something below the door. Nick told me I only have about three to seven minutes to kill as many people as possible. How fucked-up is that? This isn't a video game.

At the next room, I open the door, but it's empty. I see the back door ajar and realize they all must have run out. *Good.* But the next room is not only open, but everyone is hiding behind desks. I step into the room and begin shooting. It's surreal. I feel sick, literally. My friends are in this room. I do what I'm supposed to do because I believe what Nick said. This is important. It's life or death.

Once the stupid drill is over, I watch as everyone moves back into the room. I feel someone tug on my arm. It's Nick.

"This time, I want you to hide the gun. I'll give you a signal. At that time, I need you to shout out something like 'I'm not going to take this anymore' and begin shooting."

"Fuck," I mutter.

"I know." He pats my back and moves into the cafeteria.

I slide the gun into my pants and cover it with my shirt. In the large group, Nick explains what we did right and what we did wrong. "Getting away should be your first priority. For those of you who had no exit, you need to devise a plan to barricade your room. If there's a window to the outside, having a hammer or some type of tool on hand to break out the window is a good idea, along with a kit filled with bandages, tourniquets, or anything to stop bleeding. Tampons, feminine pads, gauze, things like that."

"Whoa," someone mutters.

Nick nods, "I agree. It gets real when you realize you need an emergency triage kit in your room."

As I listen, my eyes are on Nick. He said he'd give me a signal and he did. He reached up and pulled on his earlobe. It's my cue. At the top of my lungs, I shout, "I can't take it anymore." The group is so startled they just stare at me. When I pull out the gun, I point it into the crowd and begin shooting. I literally feel sick. I hit my best friends, all of them. The looks on their faces will forever be etched in my mind. As soon as Nick calls time, I drop the gun and run into the bathroom. My eyes are filled with tears, and nausea overtakes me. I make it in time, thankfully. I'm retching my guts out when I feel a warm hand on my back and another one pushing my hair back. "You okay?"

I squeak in surprise. It's Nick. In the women's restroom. Using the back of my hand to wipe my face, I slowly turn to face him.

"I'm sorry, Keely."

I shake my head. "No. Don't be. You're right about all of it. I'm just not cut out to shoot people."

"Good to know." He chuckles. "You okay to continue?"

I nod. "Just let me wash up. I'll be out in a minute."

When I return to the group, I'm immediately wrapped up in the arms of my friends.

"That was intense," says Sally.

"Fuckin' right," mutters Kimberly.

"Alright. That was a lesson in what to do if you're surprised by the shooter. I timed you; the entire room cleared in about five seconds. You ran. That's good. Save yourself."

Nick looks at me and smiles. A real smile. A real gorgeous smile. A smile that makes my heart beat so hard I felt it against my sternum.

Stupid, traitorous heart.

CHAPTER NINE

Nick

MY HEART IS BEATING out of my chest. It has been since she ran into the bathroom. It surprised me. I mean, if you had told me a couple of weeks ago that Keely Palmer was this damn sweet, I'd probably have laughed my ass off. The Keely I remember from the two traffic stops and even from the art class is sassy, a tad belligerent, and vapid. But I think I may have been wrong. When she said she'd die for the kids in her classroom, I wanted to pick her up, carry her out of this place, and plant her right in my living room. I wanted her with me. I wanted to protect her. Always.

"Shit." *What the hell am I saying?*

"How did your sessions go?" Captain Morgan asks as we walk to our cars.

"Intense."

"I heard. One of your shooters threw up?"

"Yep."

"This shit is real. I'm glad they took it seriously."

Me too. I don't say it, though; I merely nod.

~

IT'S FINALLY FRIDAY. "God, what a week," says Sergeant Stan Dallas, taking a drink of his beer. Raising his glass to our table, he says, "To protect and serve."

We all follow suit. "To protect and serve."

"So." I turn to my right and see Officer Amy Tompkins. She's in charge of our K-9 unit.

"So?" I give her a smirk.

"Why are you here?"

I look at the guys around the table and chuckle nervously. I know what she's asking, but I play dumb. "I was thirsty, and Sergeant Stan invited me."

The table laughs right along with me.

"No." She shakes her head. She's a little tipsy. Probably because she skipped beer in favor of something much stronger. Something amber and in a rocks glass. "Why did you leave Phoenix P.D. and come to this hellhole?"

"Hey!" a couple of the guys shout. "Fuck you, Tompkins."

"Whatever," Amy slurs. Turning back to me, she arches her brow. "Spill."

"Just needed a change of pace." I sip my beer and hope she's too drunk to keep this line of questioning going.

"Bullshit. You took a pay cut. And it's boring as fuck here."

"Hey, Amy?" Stan is making an attempt to intervene. It appears Amy isn't a fun drunk.

"What?" she snaps.

"Lay off the newbie."

"Newbie?" she scoffs. "He's older than me." Looking at me, she asks. "How old are you?"

"Thirty."

"See?" She points at me but directs her question to Stan. "He's old. I'm twenty-three."

I'm not old. Jesus. I might as well come clean and not drag this shit out. I know Stan knows the story, as does the captain. "My partner was nearly killed during a routine traffic stop."

The table is now silent and looking at me.

"We pulled over a nondescript sedan going fifteen over on a busy road." *God, I hate thinking about this.* "She jumped out before I could get the plate called in, and I didn't stop her."

They know protocol. Call in the plate. See if the car has expired plates or, worse, stolen.

"I waited in the squad car. Just as I heard them radio that the car was stolen, I looked up and watched my partner jump back suddenly." Damn, I hate retelling this story. "She, um, she jumped back when the driver pulled a gun on her."

A couple of the guys nod knowingly. It happens.

"Did the perp shoot her?"

I almost wish he had. "No. She was startled by the gun and jumped back into traffic just as a car was passing."

"Fuck!" shouts one of the other young officers. I think his name is Joel.

"The impact caused her body to be thrown into the air about twenty feet and land in front of the suspect's car. When he pulled out, he ran over her."

"Jesus," says Officer Tompkins. "She survive?"

Barely. "She did. She was in a coma for weeks. Head trauma." She'll never be the same. And I feel partially responsible. I didn't follow protocol. I was the senior officer and I didn't follow fucking protocol. "She has two kids." It took her two months to figure out who anyone was.

"Jesus, dude."

"So, that's why I'm here. A change of pace."

"A slow-as-fuck pace," mutters Tompkins.

"Exactly."

"I'm sorry, Nick."

I look over at Tompkins. She looks like she's about to cry. Her chin is wobbling. "Amy?"

"Time for Amy to go home." Stan is behind her, pulling her chair out. "She's had a bad fucking week, haven't you?"

"I have."

"I'm taking you home. Sleep it off."

"Okay, Sergeant Stan." She wraps her arm around his and walks out the door.

"That story"—I look over as one of our bicycle cops, Mark adds—"sucked." Then Mark chuckles, but it holds no humor.

"Hey." Joel slaps Mark's chest with the back of his hand. "Hot A.F. pussy at nine o'clock."

All three of us slowly rotate our heads to Joel's nine o'clock, a table filled with four women and one tall man. Keely and her friends. Damn, she looks beautiful. I haven't seen her for a couple of weeks. I suppose that's a good thing. It means she hasn't broken any laws recently.

"I call dibs on the curvy little blonde," says that fucker Mark. "I love me a spinner."

I want to punch his stupid teeth out. *A spinner?* I look over my shoulder at her, and I actually see what he means, but, damn it, I'm the only one that gets to think of her like that.

"She's mine," I growl.

"Kinda young for you, isn't she?" smirks Joel. "You like the young ones?"

"She's twenty-five." I checked. "And she's mine. As in m-i-n-e. If I hear you say one more fucking word about her, I'll end you."

Okay, where the fuck did that come from? She isn't mine. I lay my head back and close my eyes.

Why, Nick? Why?

"Sorry, man. I had no idea. You weren't paying attention to her."

"I didn't know she was here."

"What are you waiting for? Go to your sweet A.F. pussy."

"Knock it the fuck off, Joel," I spit.

"That's Joel." He points to the other guy. "*I'm* Mark."

I don't give a fuck.

I slide off my stool and start the slow trek over to Keely's table. I hope she knows how to play along.

"Hey!" shouts Mark. "What about her friends? That tall brunette is hot AF too."

I turn my head back and mutter, "Off-limits."

I'm about two feet from her table when Keely slowly turns her face toward me. When our eyes meet, she smiles at me. A real smile. A smile that makes me feel things inside that I probably shouldn't. When I'm directly in front of her, I lean down and whisper in her ear, "Play along, yeah?"

She nods, and I do something that screams, *worst idea ever*. I slide my palm up her arm and into her long, shiny, golden locks. It's down tonight. Wavy and gorgeous. Grasping a handful of her hair, I use the thumb on my other hand to press under her chin, gently, nudging it upward. Without a word, I lean down and let my lips touch hers. Goddamn, she's got soft lips.

I run my mouth over hers once, twice, then I turn my head just enough to suckle on her plump bottom lip. She makes a noise that vibrates through my lips. I take it as approval and ease my tongue inside her open mouth.

I feel warmth from her hands as they move up my chest. My shirt is pulled taut on my back thanks to the hold she's got on the front. The hand that was in her hair moves downward so I can pull her closer.

When her tongue touches mine, I nearly combust. Her

kisses become hungry. Like mine. I think I could kiss this woman for hours. Perhaps years. It's the hottest kiss of my life. I'm tempted to slide my palm down further to feel more of her when I hear it. Clapping.

Pulling away quickly, my brain returns to current day—current time. I look at Keely's friends. They're clapping and saying all sorts of encouraging things like, "You go, girl." I assume that's directed at Keely. I turn to the table of cops, and they're pretty much doing the same. I block out the rude-ass shit they're saying and look back down at Keely. She's breathing so hard her chest is moving up and down dramatically.

"You okay?"

"Oh, yeah," she says, smirking. "You really know how to surprise a girl."

I slide a piece of hair that's covering her cheek off her face. She's so damn pretty. "Sorry," I whisper. "The assholes I work with were saying things."

"Things?"

"About you."

"About me?" She says it loudly. Without a second thought, Keely steps away from me and marches over to my table. "Hey, assholes. What were you saying about me?"

They look over at me, then back to her. I'd love to save them, but they deserve whatever she dishes out.

"Nothing," Joel says like a coward.

"Nothing," she deadpans. "What about you?" she asks, pointing at Mark.

"All I said was you were hot."

Keely's tapping her foot, her little hands on her hips. "And?"

"And nothing," Mark sputters.

"*You* said more, Mark." Joel is throwing him under the bus.

They both said rude shit. "To summarize, he said you were hot and...."

Keely's face changes colors. She was pink after the kiss, but now she's fire-engine red. "And?"

Joel nods, but Mark stays still. "A spinner."

"A spinner?" She pulls her phone out of her pocket and taps away. When she's found what she's looking for, she lifts her head and glares at the two dumbasses. "There's so much wrong with that statement, assholes. First," she holds up one finger, "it's not twenty-fucking-sixteen anymore, fellas. You can't objectify women in that manner anymore. Grow the fuck up."

Mark tries to talk but Keely keeps going.

"Two. You're a cop, right?" Keely snaps out the question.

"Yeah. We both are."

"Can I get your names, please?"

She picks up a napkin and swipes a pen from a waitress passing by.

"Why do you want our names?"

"I think I'll give the chief a call and tell him all about this."

"What?" Joel seems shocked. "Why? He's not going to care. We're off duty."

"He'll care." She nods slowly. "Even off duty you represent the department, am I right?"

"Nick, dude. Tell your woman to back off."

I didn't see who asked me that, because my sole focus is on my girl. She's unbelievable.

She slowly turns to me. "Your woman?"

I move up and wrap my arm around her, giving her hip a squeeze. "*My* woman."

"Oh, Jesus," she mutters, stepping out of my arms. She looks at Joel and Mark. "I feel sorry for you two."

"Why?" scoffs Joel.

"Because you obviously don't have a clue. Women deserve respect. If you treat your women like that, guess what?"

"What?"

"They'll figure it out, wise up, and move on to a *real* man."

"Oooh, snap," says the guy she's always with. He's moved closer to the fray.

"Damn, *giiiiirl*." I hear from behind me from one of her other friends. "Harsh but true."

"They deserve it." She rolls the napkin up in a ball and tosses it into Joel's beer. "Have a nice life, pricks."

As she passes me, she pats my chest and says seductively, "Night, lover."

God, she's such a smart-ass. I love it.

CHAPTER TEN

HONEST TO GOD, I can't believe that happened last night.

He kissed me.

Nick Martelli kissed me. And it was the kiss to end all kisses. There will never be one as good as that. Ever. It contained all of the necessary ingredients to make the perfect kiss: 1) Anticipation. He moved in slowly, even whispering in my ear, which gave me chills. The good kind. 2) Lips. His were soft, gentle but also firm and investigatory. Meaning, he experimented with ways to use his lips. Sucking, nibbling, and then consuming mine.

I fan myself, because just thinking about it is making me swoon. "Okay, get it together, Keely." Next on the list? Tongue. Like his lips, his tongue was tentative yet exploratory. That was, until it met mine, and that's all she wrote. He's a master with his tongue.

Oh, shit. I wonder if he's good with his tongue in other places too.

I'm going to combust if I keep this up. The sad thing? I'm doing it in my car on the way to my life drawing class. "What if he's the model?" I say aloud as I pull out into the intersection. When I hear horns and squealing sounds, I freeze. Looking around, I see a car heading my way. It looks like it's trying to stop. I stomp my foot on the brake and squeeze my eyes closed, hoping they don't hit me. Why? Because I'm in Keeton Gustafson's fancy-ass car. Lainie would literally kill me if I wrecked this thing.

When I feel assured that there won't be contact, I slowly open my eyes. The man in the car that nearly hit mine is yelling. At me. My window is up, so I can't hear him. Good thing, because I can only imagine what he's saying. Oh, wait... I can read his lips. *"You fucking stupid cunt. Why, I ought to..."*

I wince at his words. "I'm not stupid." *He* is. The jackass. I'm raising my middle finger so I can give him a few words of my own when there's a knock on the window. Pressing the power window button down (Did I mention what a sweet-ass ride this is? Power windows. Power everything.), I peer out and see him. My man.

"Oh, hey, Nick." I give him my prettiest smile. It shows off my dimple.

"What the hell, Keely? Whose car is this?"

"Keeton's."

"Keeton? Who's Keeton?"

"Gustafson. He owns..."

"Gustafson Custom Motorcycles. I know. Why do you have his car?" Nick runs his palm over his cheek. "Never mind. Do you realize you ran a red light?"

"No way. I was stopped."

"You were, and then for some inexplicable reason, you just pulled out into traffic."

I watch as he paces back and forth. When the guy from the other car attempts to approach, Nick holds his palm up. "Back in your car, sir. I'll be there in a moment."

"But—"

"Sir," Nick says angrily. "Get back into your vehicle."

The guy mutters something and gets back into his car.

Turning back to me, Nick glares. "You're a menace."

I look up and see that statement is directed at me. "I—"

He holds his palm up to me now. "You're going to get killed, Keely. Either that or you'll kill someone else."

"I will not!" God, what an asshole. Okay. Truth? I know I was lucky back there.

"Are you okay?"

Oh, so *now* he cares? I scoff and sputter while crossing my arms over my chest.

"Pull over into that lot." Nick points to a strip mall lot to my right. "And for the love of God, pay attention to where you're going."

Okay. That's ridiculous. I'm not a bad driver. Sure, I've had a fender-bender or two, but who hasn't? I look at the fancy clock on the dash and wince. I'm going to be late. Ms. P doesn't tolerate tardiness. It can't be helped, I guess. Turning on my blinker, I drive to the lot and park next to his police cruiser. While I wait, I text Michael letting him know I'm running late. I do not tell him why. He's such a busybody. If I tell him, he'll tell everyone.

I don't have to wait long. Officer Nick Martelli stomps over to my car. "Out of the car."

"What?"

"Now."

Jesus. I push the door open, all the while muttering mean things about stupid, hot cops.

"In the squad car," the irksome man snaps.

"What!?" I screech. "You can't arrest me for *almost* getting in an accident."

"I can if you keep up this bullshit, Keely."

"You're not the boss of me." Okay, sure, so I launched into kindergarten speak, but who cares?

"I so *am* the boss of you."

I'd laugh at the way he said it, but by the look on his face, he wasn't being funny. At. All.

I step out of the vehicle, slam the door shut, and walk to his police car. Standing next to the back door, I peer inside. It's like a traveling cage in there. I know what it's like in one of those. *Oops, Let's save that story for another day.*

"In the front." Nick Bossyboots Martelli points to the passenger side.

"Fine," I growl. Stomping over to the other side of the car, I open the door and slip inside. Now *this* is cool. I don't remember much about the squad car I was in back then. I do remember I was in college, underage, and drunk as a skunk after going to a raging fraternity party that got busted. I was squished in the back with several of my girlfriends. We actually had a really good time. That was, until we woke up in the slammer, cursed with the hangover from hell. I vividly remember proclaiming, "I'm never drinking again." Ha! That's what we all say.

Nick opens his door and slides into his seat. His uniform makes funny noises as he moves in. There are some clinks from handcuffs and squeaking sounds from the leather belt and holster. I kind of like the sounds. I'm checking him out in his seated position, and I've sort of zeroed in on his crotch. Damn, the man is built.

I hear him sigh, but I can't seem to bring myself to look up at him. "Eyes up here, Keely."

Shit. Busted. I look up at his face. His cop glasses are off. I watch as he tosses them onto the dash.

"What am I going to do with you?"

Okay, there's innuendo in there. I know it. I'll play along. I mean, *he* kissed *me*, not the other way around. The ball should be in my court now, right? "Spank me?"

His reaction confuses me. He growls, slams his hand on the steering wheel, and glares at me. His chocolate brown eyes actually glare. "This is fucking serious, babe."

Babe? Ooh, that's nice. I guess it is getting serious. I stay quiet. I'm too busy trying to figure all this out.

"Are you listening to me?"

"Cool your jets, Nick. No one was hurt. I—"

Pulling off his hat, he tosses it onto the center console next to a small laptop computer.

"I'm giving you a citation."

"Another one?" Oh, my God. I can't afford another ticket.

"Another one."

"I'm going to lose my license, asshole."

"Watch it," Nick says, holding his finger up.

"Or what?" I cross my arms over my chest. Damn, I've let this get out of hand. I need to defuse the situation. I slowly uncross my arms. Reaching over, I place my palm over his forearm. "Nick?" I say ever-so-sweetly.

He turns his head, looking first down at his forearm, then back at me. He's no longer scowling, but the replacement expression isn't great. His lips are in a thin line, and his left brow is higher than his right one. I stare at his left eye, and I swear it's twitching.

In a deep, growly voice, Nick says, "If you think you're going to use your wiles to get out of this, you're crazy."

Crazy like a fox.

"No. Of course not." I've made my voice soft and soothing. "I just can't lose my license. I need to get to work." I flutter my eyelashes at him and slowly lean close to him. It's too bad the stupid computer is in the way.

"You're doing it," he says, slamming the laptop lid down. "You're using your looks and my feelings to get out of this."

Feelings? "No, I'm not. I swear." I hold my hand up and give him a three-fingered salute. "Scout's honor."

"You weren't a Scout. You grew up with four sisters. That's just bullshit."

He knows about my sisters? "Girl Scouts." Campfire Girls. Technically not the same thing, but he doesn't need to know that.

"Oh. Right." His voice has gotten softer. "Listen, Keely."

I lean in. And wait.

"I'm seriously concerned about your driving. What if you get hurt?"

"Pssshhaaw," I say, waving him off. "I won't."

"I'm more concerned with the way you're blowing this off. You could have hit someone else or worse, if that guy had t-boned your car, you'd be lucky to be alive."

"That car," I point to Keeton's ride, "is safe as hell."

Nick looks over at the car, then back at me. A scowl is back on his face. "You seeing him?" He jerks his head to the car.

Ooh, he's jealous. I could take advantage of that, but I don't want to. "No. He's with my sister. He's supposedly working on Bluebell."

"Bluebell?"

"Yeah. Bluebell. My car."

Nick chuckles, and I feel relief. "Women."

I don't know what he's talking about. I could lay into him about that sexist comment, but I won't. "So."

"I'm giving you a ticket for failure to yield."

"What!" I stomp my foot. "You're kidding me with this bull-shit? Right?"

"I'm not. And you should feel lucky I don't take you down to the station for this attitude you're giving me right now. Keep it up. It'd serve you right to lose your license."

"Well." I sniff. "That's just bullshit."

"Take what you can get here. I'm letting you off easy and not because you're cute."

Uh-huh. But I don't think cute hurts.

"Can you just write it up now? I'm late for your aunt's class."

"She's not going to like that. Want me to text her?"

"Really?"

"No," he huffs. "Serves you right."

Dick.

"I heard that." I must look shocked, because he laughs. "Gotcha."

CHAPTER ELEVEN

Nick

AFTER WRITING UP HER WARNING, against my better judgement, I hand it to her. "Promise me you'll pay better attention, drive the speed limit, and be safe?"

"I will." She holds up those three fingers again. "Promise."

Fucking Scout's honor. She's full of shit. But damn, she's cute. And hot. And sexy in her little denim cutoffs and worn tee that says, *I Became a Teacher for the Money and Fame.*

Ha. They need one of those for cops.

"So, Nick?"

"Mm?"

"What'd that kiss mean last night?"

Cutting right to the chase. I like it. The women I've dated in the past have all been about subterfuge. Shit, that question is a trap. If I say "nothing," then it sounds like I don't want to do it again. And I do. I want to do more than that. If I say, "I don't know," then that means I'm an indecisive pussy. Instead, I'm going to force the ball back into her court. "What did it mean to you?"

"Oh, I see," she says, reaching for the door handle. "I don't have time for that shit." Pushing it open, she steps out and slams it shut.

I watch with my mouth agape as she moves to her car, slides in, tosses the now crumpled ticket into the back seat, and starts her car, taking off as soon as the motor revs to life. I'm rather shocked. She's such a surprise. Keely Palmer is a no-bullshit kind of woman, and it's fucking refreshing.

Pulling out into traffic, I drive across town to the City of Page Art Center. It's where my aunt teaches part-time since she retired. It's also where Keely Palmer is just getting out of her car. I pull into the open spot next to her and watch her roll her eyes. Opening my door, I step out and walk to her. "I don't know what this is. All I know is I want to see you."

She raises her arms. "Here I am. You're seeing me."

"Alright." I step closer. "I want you in my bed. From there, we can figure it out."

Keely nods. "Sounds good. Text me your address. I'll be over later." She steps around me. "What time do you get off?"

I'm tempted to say "every time I think of you" but I don't. "Five."

"I'll be there at six." She walks toward the Art Center door. "Oh, and Nick?"

"Yeah."

"Be ready."

Fuck. I'm ready now. I smile and wave because I'm pretty sure my throat seized up. The woman is a siren. I guess that's appropriate for a cop.

~

I RACED home after my shift to get ready for Keely. I showered and did my best to pick up my house. Years in the army taught me how to keep my shit tidy, but that doesn't mean it was spic-n-span. I quickly wiped down my counters, tossed my dishes into my dishwasher, and ordered food. Since I wasn't sure what she liked, I went crazy and ordered a bunch of different things from Giovanni's, the best fucking Italian food I've ever eaten. Surely she likes Italian. I even ordered a meatless entrée in case she's a vegetarian.

When my doorbell rings, I smile. She's five minutes early. I check myself in the mirror. I didn't want to dress up and look like an idiot, so I chose my nicest jeans and a gray army T-shirt. It makes me feel confident for some reason. With no time to put on shoes, I step to the door, opening it up to a guy with two large brown paper sacks. Dinner.

I pay the man and give him a decent tip. Moving into the kitchen, I pull everything out of the bags and spend a good ten minutes trying to figure out how to arrange them so they look nice and they're not just piles of Styrofoam containers. I finally just line them up in two rows and call it good. Reaching into my fridge, I pull out a bottle of blush wine for her and a bottle of beer for myself. I set both on the counter along with two plates, silverware, and napkins. I stare down at my spread, making sure I've got everything I need.

Nodding in approval, I step back out into my small living room and look at the door, then at the wall clock.

"Six fifteen." Hmm, weird. She's late. I roll my eyes. Of course she's late. It's Keely. I told her to slow down and take care when she drives. I bet she's just being extra careful. I sit down on my sofa and pick up the remote. I could watch a little news until she gets here.

I check the clock every five minutes until six thirty.

Where the hell is she? Maybe I should call her.

I reach into my back pocket for my phone, but it's not there. Jumping up, I practically jog into my bedroom. Searching the dresser and nightstand, I move to the bathroom. "There it is." I must have left it on the counter before I showered. Picking it up, I see one missed text message. I'd done as she asked and sent her a text message with my address.

Keely: Something came up. I can't make it. Sorry.

An overwhelming sense of disappointment slams into my chest. "Fuck." I was really looking forward to tonight. And not just the sex. My dick's been hard since I saw her today, but that's not why. I really wanted to get to know her. I decide to reply.

Me: I hope everything is okay. No worries. Sweet dreams.

Before I can think better of it, I hit send. Sure, it sounds like a pussy wrote that text, but for some reason, I don't give a fuck.

CHAPTER TWELVE

KEELY

I COULDN'T DO IT. I couldn't go on a date with a cop. First of all, my court date is in three days. I need to prepare myself for that because a) I can't afford those tickets and b) I won't be able to face him and fight for myself if I've slept with him because I know the minute I sleep with him I'll be a goner.

The other reason rests solely in the hands of my twin sister, Violet. She's the reason I despise the police.

What? You want to know why? Sorry, that's not my story to tell. But I will say this. When we needed the cops the most, they did nothing. Abso-fucking-lutely nothing. Worse than nothing. They made shit worse. God, I fucking hate cops. And if I'm smart, I'll lump one Nick Martelli right in with them.

LEAVE it to me to have my court date on April Fool's Day.

Because that's what I am. A fool to think that Nick Martelli would have a sympathetic bone in his body. Spoiler alert, he doesn't.

The minute I walked into the traffic court offices; I knew I was screwed. Not only was Nick there, but he brought friends—two other cops. Two other cops I recognize because they'd let me off with warnings. They, at least, had feelings. But, oh no. Not hard-ass Nick Martelli. He's heartless.

Nevertheless, I check in with the clerk and await my time in front of the traffic court judge to plead my case, all the while regretting this entire decision to try to fight the system—fight the *man*. I should have thought this through. I should have let my brain go back six years to the shit-show that was Violet's experience with Tucson P.D. It didn't matter what we did back then, they weren't going to help her. And while my traffic tickets are *nothing* like what Violet went through, I still feel the same helplessness—like it's me against them. With that said, I'm not about to take this lying down. If there's any chance I can win even part of my case, I have to try. Besides, I'm broke and these fines are insane. "Fucking cops," I mutter aloud.

"Now, now. We're not so bad."

I didn't even see him approach. Nick must have snuck up on me. Not to mention he was eavesdropping. Sure, I was only talking to myself, but it counts. "Yeah, you are."

I haven't looked at him yet. Not in the eye. I did notice he was wearing dark slacks, black, I'd guess, and a button-down shirt in a sort of buttery yellow color. I take that opportunity to look at him, and I want to swallow my tongue. The man looks almost as delicious in his off-duty clothes as he does in uniform. He's hot as sin either way. The shirt somehow brings out a gold hue in his brown eyes. I scan down his body and see his pants are a dark brown. He's wearing brown leather loafers with socks, thankfully—I don't like that no-socks look that some guys prefer

—and a matching belt. I do my best to keep my eyes off his crotch, because we're in court. That would be wrong.

"You look...." He pauses before saying, "What's with the sexy schoolgirl look?"

"I'm a school teacher. It's how we dress." *Duh!* Okay, so it's not really how we dress. If I wore a skirt this short to my classroom, I'd have little heads trying to get a look at my white cotton panties. So, yeah, I'm wearing a plaid skirt, knee high socks, and a white blouse like a parochial schoolgirl, and kitten-heeled Mary Jane shoes. I thought it made me look innocent.

I could swear Nick was making a growling noise. "You could wear that to my house. Tonight."

"Pervert."

I'm about to lay into him when I hear my name echoing through the hallowed halls of the courthouse: "Keely Palmer?"

"That's me." Grabbing my file folder filled with my documents, I step around Nick and move toward the clerk.

"You're up," says the clerk.

I make my way into the courtroom. There are twenty or thirty other people in the room. The clerk points me to an open seat at the back. "Judge'll call you up when it's your turn."

I nod. I'm so nervous. I wish I'd gotten Violet to come with me, but this is my fight.

I wait forever. Literally. I swear I've waited hours for my name to be called. When it's my turn, I step in front of the judge. I'm asked to raise my right hand and pledge an oath to tell the truth.

"I do," I say somberly. Of course, I do. I mean, this shit is getting real.

This is scary. I'm shaking like a leaf. I'm barely making out what the judge is telling me. When I finally realize he's called Nick and his sidekicks into the room, I feel a sense of relief. Nick's here. *He'll* help me.

NICK DIDN'T HELP ME. On the contrary, he, along with his cop buddies, threw me under the proverbial bus. By the time they were done, the judge had to decide whether or not I was going to get the book thrown at me. And by book, I mean pay the fines. Even after I explained how I was late for class and distracted by, you know, life things. It was no good.

As luck would have it—his, not mine—the judge ruled against me. He told me to leave the courtroom and make payment arrangements with the clerk. I guess that's one good thing. I got to make payment arrangements, which I needed, because now, on top of the three heinous ticket amounts, I had to pay court costs.

People. I am so disgusted with the legal system right now. No, honestly, I'm disgusted with myself. I wasn't prepared. I didn't do my homework. If I had to do it all over again... What the hell am I saying? I never want to do this again.

Now I'm waiting in line to pay my fines. And from the looks of the length of said line, I'd say every single person who appeared today is paying.

What a fucking scam.

After I finally get my turn, I make payment arrangements, get my receipt, and hurry out of the building. I hope I never set foot in that place again. I reach into my purse to get my phone. I need a taxi because I still don't have Bluebell back. I'm about to hit the number for the local service when I feel warm air on my neck and ear.

"So, you want to come over tonight?"

He can't be serious.

As slowly as possible, I rotate until I'm facing him. He's bent at the waist, so we're nearly eye-to-eye. "You think after that bullshit in there I'm going to fuck you?"

He looks up like he's thinking about it, then back at me. "Hate fucks are fun."

Oh, God. They are. They're super fun. I'm about to fall for it when I get wise. "Nope."

"Why not?" Nick actually sounds a little whiny.

"You're a cop. I can't do cops."

"What did I ever...." He smartly stops talking but only for a second. "Okay. I get why you're pissed, but I did it for your own good."

What am I? Five? "You're an asshole." I hit send and wait for the service to answer. When they do, I say, "I need a ride."

"Hang up."

Ignoring him, I'm about to give them the address when he pulls the phone out of my hand and hits end.

"Nick. Goddammit."

"I'll drive you. Where to?"

I was going to go back to school, but it's nearly three now. I spent my entire personal day at the courthouse, which sucks, because personal days are precious. We only get two per year, and I like to save them for emergencies. Using this one today was a fucking waste.

Fine. Without a word, I follow him to a newer SUV. It's pearly white with a tan leather interior. Ideal for the Arizona heat. Nick holds the door for me, so I slide in and see he's got heated *and* cooled seats. Again, great for AZ.

"Where to?"

I give him my address and sit silently as he drives. Turning on the radio, I'm amused to hear country music. I wouldn't have taken him for a country fan. I like it though. I like all kinds of music.

As I tap along to the song, he asks, "You like country?"

I shrug. I'm still not going to talk to him. Sure, it's juvenile, but so what?

At my apartment complex, I point him to a spot in front of my building. I quickly open the door and slide out. Without looking back, I walk as fast as my short legs will carry me up the three flights of steps to my landing. I hear him behind me. I don't know what he thinks he's doing.

At my door, I've got my keys in hand, ready to unlock it, but Nick takes them, nudging me aside. Once I hear a click, I push the door open and walk in without a word. Dropping my purse on the small table next to my front door, I step into my kitchen for some water. From the corner of my eye, I watch Nick examine my apartment. It's not much, but I've done what I can to make it cute. Lainie's added a few touches since she moved in with me after her divorce. I don't think she'll be here much longer, sadly. I've enjoyed having her around.

"That's quite a lamp." Nick chuckles as he makes himself at home. He's sitting on my one and only sofa-slash-loveseat.

The lamp was one of Lainie's additions. It was my mom's. Lainie got it on her sixteenth birthday along with a letter from her. Shit. My nose is starting to tingle. Thinking of the things our mom left for Dad to give each of us on our sixteenth birthdays still brings tears to my eyes. I got her music box with the spinning ballerina. God, I loved that thing. I played with it nearly every day. Mom told me I could have it someday if I took "very good care of it." I did. I was always careful with it. My chin starts to quiver thinking about her letter.

"Baby," Nick says soothingly. "Don't cry."

I shake it off. "It's not about you or the tickets."

"Why, then?"

I do what I can to get my feelings in check. Moving into the living room, I stand in front of him. "None of your business." Because it isn't.

I think he's about to open his trap again, but I shush him by placing my finger over his mouth. Sliding a knee onto the couch,

I do the same with the other one until I'm straddling him. Now that he's here, a hate fuck sounds sort of nice.

"Keely."

"No words. Just feels."

"Feels?" He chuckles. That is, until I slide my palm down his abdomen and over his rock-hard cock. Then he shuts the hell up.

About damn time.

CHAPTER THIRTEEN

Nick

I STARE in near disbelief as the gorgeous and spontaneous Keely Palmer grinds herself on my crotch. I've a mind to carry her to the bedroom to move this forward, but to be honest, it's the hottest thing I've ever seen. As soon as I shut my mouth, Keely runs her palm down my chest to my dick. She wraps her fingers around me, as much as she can, and begins sliding her small hand up and down. Even though this is all happening over my trousers, it feels fucking great. It's been a while for me, so any contact from a hand other than my own is welcome.

Sadly, she removes her hand far too soon. When she slides forward until her pussy replaces her hand, I move with her. As we grind our hips forward and back, she slowly begins to unbutton her pristine white blouse. The one she wore with the tiny plaid skirt and white knee socks.

Now, I'm not a pervert. I like women my own age but damn if the sexy schoolgirl thing didn't work for her. I spent the entire time in the courtroom wondering what she had underneath the skirt. Was it a thong? Or white cotton panties? My God, who knew the thought of white cotton granny panties could make my cock so hard?

As she grinds on me, she slowly opens up her shirt to reveal a sweet white bra, and I slide my palms up her thighs, beneath the skirt to the motherland. Cupping her, I run my palm between her legs, and I'm pleased to announce the undies are cotton. I don't know the color just yet, but I will. As though in slow motion, I watch as Keely reaches back to unhook her bra, holding my breath as she slides the straps down until all is revealed.

"Shit." She's beautiful.

Her palms slide up from her rib cage like she's going to do my job for me.

"Mine," I growl.

Keely starts to laugh, and I ignore her because my focus is on those. I remove my hands from her undies. The color will have to wait, because her breasts are spectacular. Perfect. On the small side, but round and perky. Not surprising for someone as compact as she is. Her nipples are the prettiest shade of pink and pebbled. I palm both of them without another thought. Keely moans and lets her head drop back, all the while still moving on my lap. I lean forward and run my tongue over her hard nipple. *Jesus.* She tastes so good. What is on her skin? Candy? So fucking sweet.

I do the same to her other breast as my hand squeezes and plucks the neglected breast. I can tell Keely likes it, and it's not because she's saying things like, "Yes, Nick. That feels so good." No, it's because the pace of her thrusting hips has doubled. She's chasing her orgasm, and I intend to help it along. Reaching down, I slide my palm up her leg and let my fingers slip beneath the elastic, moving to her slit. She's so damn wet, and her clit is hard and reaching out for attention. I slide my middle finger over the hard nub and circle it. Once it's between my fingers, I say, "Come for me, Keely." I pinch her there and she explodes.

"Oh, my God, Nick," Keely says, still moving on top of me. I need for her to stop or I'll blow in my pants. That's not where I want to release. Wrapping my hands around her waist, I lift her. She wraps her legs around my back and her hands around my neck.

"Bedroom," I say huskily.

"Down the hallway. Last door on the left."

I march us both down the hallway into her bedroom. Moving to her full-size bed, I set her down. Turning, I search for a light switch. I stop once I see the glow from a lamp on the bedside table.

Turning back to the bed, I smile. She's in the middle of the bed, kneeling with her hands resting on her thighs. "You're beautiful."

"Thank you," she says rather shyly. Not like the confident sex kitten on the couch just a minute ago.

I begin to unbutton my dress shirt and can't help noticing her eyes are on my dick. It's hard to miss, since I'm tenting my trousers to their limit. She remains quiet as I slide off my shirt, unbuckle my belt, and let my pants slide down my legs. Kicking those away, I remove my socks, left in only my boxers.

I take one step toward her when she nods at my cock. "Off. Take those off."

I'm not about to argue. I push the boxers down to the floor and kick them away somewhere into the room.

"Wow."

I smirk, because why not? Grasping my cock, I run my hand up and over the head. I'm dripping with need, and with the way she's looking at me, at it, it's not lessening.

"What do you want, babe?"

"You." She's still staring at me as I play with myself. "I want you to fuck me." She moves up until she's on her knees. It gives me a view of her body. She's curvy and soft like I imagined. Placing her hands down on the bed, she rotates until her ass is in front of me. Looking back over her shoulder, she smiles. "Condoms in the nightstand, lover."

I can't take my eyes off the sight of her plump little ass. From my vantage point, I can see how pink and wanting her pussy is. Reaching over, I open the drawer and grab a condom. In seconds, I'm sheathed. Placing my knee on the bed, I slide my palm over the porcelain skin of her bottom. Her skin is so fucking soft. I grasp her around her waist and tug gently, urging her backward to bring her closer to me. Placing my cock at her entrance, I mumble, "You ready?"

"So ready. Fuck me, Nick."

I thrust in hard and nearly black out. I see stars and feel euphoric. "Holy shit, Keely."

"Do I feel good?" she asks, panting.

"Fuck, yes." She's squeezing my cock so tight, I'm afraid to move. But when her ass wiggles in front of me, I know I've got to.

"Hard and fast, Nick."

"As you wish." I pull almost all the way out and slam home again. Home. It's a good way to think of this. I never want to leave this place. Ever. I begin fucking her in earnest, all the while listening to her.

She's begging me not to stop. When I swivel my hips and move down slightly, her words come out at a fast clip. "Right there. Don't move from right there. Harder."

I live to serve, so I do just that until I feel her squeeze the fuck out of my dick. Leaning closer to her back, I'm able to nibble on the side of her neck and earlobe.

"Yours is the sweetest pussy I've ever had, babe." I move in and out as many times as I possibly can. "You're tight."

"Because your cock is huge," Keely pants.

Several thrusts more, and I explode inside of her. Leaning over her, I move her blonde ponytail away from her back and kiss her neck. I kiss across to one shoulder, then to her neck. "You okay?" I ask in her ear.

"Never better." She moves forward, separating us.

As we slide apart, I stare down at the spot we used to share. My dick is softening beneath the condom. "Bathroom?" I ask rolling it off.

Without looking at me, she points behind her. "Down the hall near the living room."

I missed it when I walked us back here. My mind was on other things, I guess. In the bathroom, I tie off the rubber and wrap it in a tissue before tossing it into the small trash can. As I wash my hands, I glimpse myself in the small vanity mirror. I look tired and completely blissed out. Maybe I'll be able wrap her up in my arms and sleep for a bit, but that thought is gone the second I see her move past the bathroom door. Still nude, I step out and follow her into her kitchen.

"You'd better get dressed. My sister will be here soon, so you need to be gone."

What? I'm staring at the back of her head as water pours from the faucet to a glass. "You kicking me out, babe?"

"Yep. I don't want my sister to see you here."

"I'm your dirty secret?"

She turns to face me. Arching her brow, she smirks. "Absolutely."

Fuck. This isn't turning out the way I'd hoped. Not at all the way I'd hoped. "Yeah. Alright." Moving down the hallway, I search the bedroom for my clothes. After dressing, I go back into the living room. Keely's curled up on the couch with a book in her hand. She's not looking at me.

"No goodbye kiss?"

Shaking her head, all she says is, "See ya."

What the fuck? I've never been booted after sex. It's always been the other way around. I hightailed it out of wherever I was. This is unfamiliar ground for me. I don't like it. At all.

"Sure. Yeah. See ya," I say, opening her front door. "I'll call you."

I pause, expecting her to say something like, "Sure. Great," but I get nothing. Stepping out onto the landing, I look left and right in an attempt to get my bearings, then jog down the steps to my car. Once inside, I stare up at her door. I'm still reeling from the sex. It's been a mere ten minutes since I came inside her, and my body is still humming. I'm fucking confused.

Keely Palmer is different. She's a riddle wrapped up in an enigma. I've heard that expression before and I've never once considered its meaning. No other explanation fits her better than that.

Walking down the steps to my car, I think about what happened. How hot it was. *And Wait. She had condoms in her nightstand?* I hadn't even given that a moment's thought until right now. Does that mean what I think it means? Is she seeing someone else? Or could there be more than one man in her life?

"Fuck."

CHAPTER FOURTEEN

KEELY

I WATCH my front door close slowly. When it clicks shut, I drop the book I wasn't really reading to the floor. Then I let myself fall face first onto my sofa.

What the hell did I just do?

I know what I just did. I fucked a cop. I went against everything I believe in by fucking Nick Martelli. In my own bed, for Christ's sake. Now I'll have to burn everything.

Not really. I won't take it to that extreme. Hell, I may even sleep on those sheets tonight. His scent won't be there. He barely set foot on the mattress and sheets. Just his legs.

A shiver runs through my body thinking about the sex. It was hot and fast. From behind too, one of my favorite positions. I should have thought better of it once I got a look at his massive cock. Jesus. I'm surprised I could take it. I guess when there's a will, there's a way. I snort at myself. Why not? I'm deliriously sated and spent. He made me come twice. That's one more than any other guy has been able to coax out of me. And I've never come during intercourse unless there were other elements at play, like fingers—my own. Nope, he did it just by moving around and swiveling his hips.

"Fuck." I grumble just as the front door opens to a smiling Lainie. Behind her is her man, Keeton.

"Hey, Keels."

"Hey, boo." I chuckle. "And Lainie." I love to give Keeton shit. The guy is intimidating to say the least, but he seems to get my humor.

He grunts in response, then asks, "You want to go to Murphy's tonight?"

"Hells, yeah!"

After all that with Nick, I need a drink. Or five.

"Cool." Keeton turns to Lainie. "Babe, I'll pick you up at seven." Turning to me, he adds, "I'll drive my truck so you can ride with us."

He usually rides one of his motorcycles.

"Okay," I say with a smile. "Hey, Keet. When do I get my effing car back?"

"It'll be done by the end of the week. I'll drop it off here."

Thank fuck. I'm totally screwed without a car.

"You need a loaner?"

"No. I can last another four days." Michael's just going to have to keep chauffeuring me to school and back for a while longer. He'll be my car bitch. *Ha!*

I watch as Lainie leans in to kiss him. I turn my head away, because I'm not a creeper. I give them privacy as needed because my big sister is in love and no one deserves it more than her.

As soon as the door shuts, Lainie turns to me. "So, what's wrong?"

"Huh?" Damn, the woman is perceptive. I shake my head. "Nothing."

"You had court today?"

Oh, shit. I forgot. "I lost. Had to pay my tickets plus court costs."

"Oh, Keels," Lainie coos. I can tell she feels bad but not as bad as I do. "Do you need money?"

"Nah. I'm on a payment plan. I'm good."

"You sure? I'd be happy to give it to you."

I smile at my sister. "I know. Thanks for the offer."

I stand up from the couch. I'm suddenly starving. I guess it makes sense; I haven't eaten since my oatmeal this morning, and sex burns lots of calories. I'll have a snack—save some space for Murphy's wings later. In the kitchen, I search the cupboards for something that sounds appetizing. Locating an old box of granola bars, I tear one open and bite.

"So, what else is bothering you?"

How the hell? "Nothing." I laugh. It's forced. "Swear."

"Uh-huh."

The truth is, if I'm going to tell someone about my tête-à-tête with a cop, it has to be Violet. She's the reason I've got such negative feelings about law enforcement. I think it would hurt her to know I broke my solemn vow to her. I just can't. Not right now. She's still so fragile.

She's always been the shy twin. We're opposites in more ways than looks, but since *it* happened, she's been even more introverted, more guarded. It sucks, because she wasn't shy with me before. She and I always had fun together. I could make her laugh and talk her into doing things that were out of her comfort zone. Like going to different colleges, for example. That was a big one. I thought it'd be good for us to separate. I wanted my independence, and I figured it'd do Violet good to spread her wings, not rely on me to help her make friends—that kind of bullshit. Really, it was a selfish endeavor. *I* wanted to be known as just Keely for once. Not as one half of a set of twins. Violet reluctantly agreed. That's why she went to the University of Southeast Arizona in Tucson and I went to Arizona State in Tempe. Our cities were driving distance from each other, about an hour and a half, but far enough away we could live separate lives.

God, I'm such a selfish asshole. I practically forced her into it. I feel responsible. That's why I need to keep my promise. I owe it to her.

CHAPTER FIFTEEN

Nick

IT'S BEEN a week since we had sex in her apartment. Since then, I've attempted to call her twice—no answer—and I've sent her four text messages. Nothing risqué or even intrusive. Just checking on her, asking how she was doing. She replied once with only a cursory "Hi, I'm good."

What the fuck? She didn't even inquire after me. Who does that? I had my dick inside her. And that's all I get? What happened to common courtesy?

"Yo! Nick. Man, what's up? You look like somebody killed your cat."

"I don't have a cat." I wish I did. At least someone would be happy to see me. Wait. Cats don't give a shit. Just like fucking Keely Palmer.

CHAPTER SIXTEEN

IT'S BEEN over a week since *The Sex* with Nick Martelli. Yes, I've given it its own title. *The Sex.* I'd love to tell you that I haven't been thinking about it. Him. But I have. I don't believe I mentioned it before, but *The Sex* with Nick was unbelievable. It may be clichéd to say this, but he was the best lay I've ever had. Hands down. Everything about it was next-level hot. It was the perfect mix of hot animal sex, dirty talk, and a little sweetness thrown in for good measure. The perfect sex-storm.

"Shit."

I want it again. And again.

He's tried to call a couple of times, but I hit the decline button on my phone, preventing him from even leaving me a message. I don't want to hear his voice. He sent several text messages too. I finally replied to one, but I kept it simple. I needed time to think. To process.

That process has resulted in a lot of waffling this week. One minute I tell myself I deserve hot sex even if it *is* with a cop. The other minute, I remind myself that family—sisterhood—trumps men. Sisters before misters and all that crap.

I've considered sitting down with Violet. Having a little heart-to-heart because I know she'd understand. Hell, she'd probably encourage me. That's the kind of person she is. Selfless.

Yeah, Keely! Unlike you, you selfish bitch.

Violet would understand, because she's the sweetest one of our Palmer bunch. She'd never ask me to deny myself. She might even like Nick Martelli. But, deep down, I don't think she'd trust him. Hell, I'm not sure *I* could ever trust him. Not entirely. And rule number one? You've got to trust your person.

No way.

I can't say those words—two of the most important words in the Palmer language.

"What the fuck!?" I yell out loud in my car.

I can't be thinking Nick Martelli is the one?!

Luckily, I'm alone in Bluebell on my way to life drawing so no one can hear me. If they did, they'd think I'd lost my marbles. First there's the talking to myself, which everyone does. *Everyone.* The other reason? The *one?* Ugh. He's not *the one,* because 1) my one would never be a cop, and 2) my one would never be prettier than me.

I snort at that one. I'm just kidding. Not about the pretty part. Nick Martelli is way prettier than me. I don't care about that. I just can't fathom that I'd be attracted to someone like Nick. He's too perfect. It'd never last. He'd figure out what a fucking hot mess I was and then he'd be gone.

"Just like that." I snap my fingers.

No. I need to remain steadfast in my promise to Violet. The

last thing I want to do is hurt my sister like that. She means the world to me. If I end up alone with a house full of cats, I'd be okay with that as long as she's happy. That's all that matters.

I attempt to clear my head as I pull into the Art Center parking lot. The first car I recognize belongs to Michael. Next to his is a pearl-colored SUV.

"Nooooo," I whine. I do not need this.

I'm tempted to back right out of the lot and head for the mall when I see another familiar vehicle filled with three other friends. I park next to Michael and walk to class with Sally, Julia, and Kimberly.

"Do you think that hot as hell cop will ever model again?" Sally sounds a little too excited for my taste.

I want to say, "I hope not." But I keep my feelings to myself. I know he's here. His SUV is in the lot.

As soon as we cross the threshold to the class, the first person I see is Nick. He's sitting on a stool, chatting with his aunt. The good news? He's not wearing a robe; instead, he's in his street clothes. My God, the man looks great in everything, even a simple pair of jeans and a T-shirt. It's almost not fair to the rest of mankind the way his plain black tee hugs his pecs and muscly arms.

I search for Michael. Spotting him in our usual spot, I walk the long way around the room—as far away from Nick Martelli as I can get.

"Hey, biatch," I say with a bright smile.

"Me? You're the biatch."

"I know." I quickly set up my area in anticipation of the lesson for today.

"Yoo-hoo, Ms. Priscilla?" Michael raises his hand and waves it frantically.

Brown-noser.

"Yes, Michael?"

"Is *Nicholas* going to model for us today?" Muttering just loud enough for me to hear, he adds, "Please say yes, please say yes."

I laugh. I can't help it. The guy cracks me up.

"Unfortunately not, boys and girls."

I love it when she calls us that.

"He's on duty in a little bit. He was nice enough to give me a lift, since my car wouldn't start and I was running late." She turns to Nick. "Right, Nicholas?"

"Right." He nods, then smiles at the group. I swear half the women (and one man) practically faint. Myself included, if I'm being honest.

"Instead, we have Tiffany modeling today for our first fully nude session."

"Fully nude?" I squeak to my friends. "I'm not ready for that."

I watch as some chick named Tiffany walks out of the same room Nick was in on the day he modeled. She's young. If she's twenty-one, I'd be shocked. I guess she'd have to be at least eighteen or else she couldn't model nude, right? Tiffany's got long blonde hair that's loose down her back. Strutting out to the center of the room, she immediately unties the belt around her waist and drops it to the ground.

"Holy shit," Kimberly mutters. "She obviously doesn't eat carbs."

"Or food." I grunt.

I'm expecting Ms. P to scold her for getting naked like that, but she says nothing. The person who does speak, instead, is our model. To Nick. Turning to face him, hand on her nonexistent hip, she says, "Nick. We should totally model at the same time. We'd look amazing together."

Ugh. Excuse me? My eyelashes start to flutter furiously as I watch their interaction.

"Slut." It comes out sounding like a cough. Michael does his best to disguise it, but we all know what he said.

I glare at Michael, because, *hello*, that's not cool. Turning my attention back to the woman talking to my man, I see Nick staring at Tiffany. How could he not? She's perfect. Tall, slim, and pretty. I bet *she* wouldn't be stupid enough to kick him out of her apartment after he gave her the fuck of her life.

My eyes are trained on the two of them as I watch the scene unfold. Holding my breath, I wait for Nick's response.

"I don't do nude modeling."

Tiffany shrugs her narrow shoulders. "You could wear your briefs. *I'll* be nude."

I can't see her face, but she's smirking, I know she is. Just the tone of her voice sounds smirky.

Nick's eyes flick to me, then back to her. "Uh."

What? He can't figure out a way to say no? Well, I can!

"That's a no, boo."

Fuck! I said that? I said that.

Shit. Shit. Shit.

My four besties are staring at me. I feel their eyes burning holes in me.

Tiff slowly turns to face me, her hand still on her twenty-four-inch waist. "Oh? And why is that?"

Why *is* that? I look over at Nick, hoping he's going to help me out. One of his dark brows is up, and the other is low while one side of his mouth is raised in an Elvis-style smirk. Is he sneering at me?

I think as quickly as I can. "His girlfriend wouldn't like it. Right, Nick?"

"Girlfriend?" More than one person repeats the word. Most sounding quite disappointed.

"My girlfriend?" Nick deadpans.

I nod, because I can't figure out what to say next.

Nick's eyes move from me to Tiffany then back to me. His eyes stay on me as he responds, "She's right. My girl wouldn't like it."

If I could describe the expression on his face right this second, I'd say it was a cross between more pissed than a startled rattler and about to laugh his ass off. Figure that one out, would ya?

"Well." Ms. P claps her hands. "Now that that's settled, let's get started. Tiffany, have a seat on the wooden chair for me, dear."

"The wooden chair?" she whines.

"Yes, my dear. The wooden chair."

Stomping her foot like a petulant child, she moves toward the wooden chair. I do my best to keep my eyes on Ms. P and the center of the room, but I can't help looking up when I see a black T-shirt moving in my direction. I know he's heading my way. I know it. And there's nothing I can do to stop him.

I feel him before I hear him. With his hand on my shoulder, he leans down from behind. "How's my girlfriend doing today?" His breath is warm on my earlobe and neck.

I nod just enough for him to see. "Good."

His lips touch the lobe of my ear, and my nipples stand at attention.

"We need to talk. My house. Tonight. Eight o'clock. Don't be late."

I nod, because I don't dare say a word. I've already said too much in front of a room full of people. Damn stupid big mouth.

I guess I should be happy. There's a chance I get to have Nick Martelli again.

The minute he's far enough away from me, Sally leans in. "I think little Miss Palmer has some explaining to do."

"Def. Some serious fucking explaining," mutters Michael. "And we want *all* the deets."

"Yep." I knew this would happen. Once they know, everyone will know. They're almost as blabby as my sisters. Almost.

CHAPTER SEVENTEEN

Nick

IF SHE THINKS I'm going to fuck her again, she's got another thing.... Oh, who am I kidding? She's probably right. But not before we have a little heart-to-heart. I hate this ghosting bull-shit. And kicking me out immediately after amazing sex is a hard no for me. I expect cuddling afterwards.

Shit. What the fuck am I talking about? It's not about cuddling, necessarily. I just didn't appreciate getting kicked out of bed like that. It left me feeling a little used. *A lot* used.

NOT GOING TO LIE. When I hear the knock on my front door, I'm a tad surprised. I thought for sure she'd send a text canceling tonight, but she didn't. I look around my space and smile. It looks good. It even smells okay. I lit a couple of scented candles Aunt P made for me.

When I get to the door, I peek out through the hole in the door. She's running her fingers through her long blonde hair. She's got it down, and thanks to my porch light, I can see how silky it is. Flipping the deadbolt, I pull the door open and step aside.

"Keely," I say with as little emotion as possible. I don't want her to know how happy I am to see her. Besides, I pulled the tee out of my jeans, so I'm covered. "Welcome." I gesture toward my living room. "Come on in."

She steps over the threshold, and I can't help noticing she's changed her clothes from this afternoon. She was in denim cutoffs and a tank earlier. Now, she's in a short white summer dress. The top is sitting off her shoulders, showing a lot of skin. A lot of soft, tanned skin. At the waist, it flares out a little bit and stops a few inches above her knees. She's also wearing some kind of high-heeled sandal that gives the impression she's much taller than she really is. She looks amazing.

"Nice place," she says as she sits on my sectional sofa.

It is a nice place. It's a ranch-style bungalow. There are three good-sized bedrooms and two full bathrooms. Plenty of room for me and for my family when and if I ever have one.

"Thanks."

I shut the door and flip the lock. Habit. Page is a very safe place, but I'm used to Phoenix, I guess. "Care for something to drink?"

"Sure."

I wait for her to tell me what she wants. When she says nothing more, I provide her with a list of options. "I've got wine, beer, soda, diet soda, and orange juice."

"Wine, please. White, if you've got it."

"Be right there." I pour her a glass of white and myself some red. Making my way back to the living room, I see she's gotten up. She's looking at some photos I've got hanging up around the room.

"This your mom?" She points to a picture of my mom when she was in her twenties.

"It is. It was."

"She's beautiful." Her head turns to me quickly. "Wait. Was?"

"She died when I was eighteen."

"How?"

"Car accident." I pause, not knowing why I want to tell her more. "She hung on for several weeks."

"Oh, Nick." Keely steps toward me, arms raised. I should bat them away, but I'm not going to deny myself a little pity and some physical contact from Keely Palmer. Her little arms around me feel fucking great. "I'm so sorry." Her voice is soft and sincere.

"Me too, babe." I run my palm up and down her back. "It's why I'm so hard on you about your driving."

She pulls back and looks up at me warily. "Oh?"

"She was speeding. Lost control of her car."

"I'm sorry about your mom, Nick, I really am, but that has nothing to do with me. I'm a great driver."

I snort because it's ridiculously funny. "Right." I move to the couch and sit, picking up my wine in the process.

"I am!" She looks defiant in her stance. Legs apart, hands on hips.

I hold up my palm to calm her. "Fine. Let's not talk about that." *Instead, let's talk about why you keep blowing me off.*

Appearing relieved, Keely walks around my coffee table and sits at the furthest end of the sofa. "I'm sorry about your mom."

"I'm sorry about yours too."

Keely blinks at me.

"Aunt Priscilla."

"Oh, right. She knew my mom."

"She told me about your sisters and said your dad is a 'good man.'" I use air quotes.

"He's the best." Keely smiles for the first time since walking into the place. "What about *your* dad?"

She seems sincerely interested, but I still scoff. "Left the week after the funeral. I haven't seen him since."

"Oh, no." She's got that damn sad face again. "He must have been devastated."

Fuck, no. I'm not going there. "Don't feel sorry for him. He made his choice. He's a fucking coward."

Keely's eyes grow round and somewhat buggy. "Sorry," she says.

"No. Don't be sorry. *I'm* sorry. I shouldn't have snapped at you. He's..." I run my fingers through my hair. "He's just not in my life. I haven't heard from him in twelve years."

"You're thirty?" she asks with a squeak.

"And you're twenty-five." Before she has a chance to ask, I add, "Your driver's license."

"Right."

The two of us remain quiet for several minutes. I watch her sip her wine as I sip mine. It's not uncomfortable, but I wouldn't call it comfortable either. I need to ask her some things, but I'm not sure where to start.

"So, about today. At class. When I intervened between you and Tiffany."

Good. She started. "Yeah?"

"I'm sorry."

I don't want her to be sorry. I want her to tell me why she did it. "Why did you do it?"

"Well...." Keely sips from her glass and fidgets in her seat. "Uh...."

I'm starting to enjoy her discomfort. "Yes?" I'm smirking on the inside.

Finally, she says, "I just thought you needed help."

"Help?"

"Yeah. I could tell you didn't want to model with her." Before I can say anything, Keely mumbles, "Not that she'd care. Could she have been any more obvious?"

"It's true. I was uncomfortable, but I was more than capable of handling that."

"It took you long enough," Keely mumbles again.

"You know I can hear you, right?"

"Look." Keely sets her wineglass down. "It was inappropriate for her to practically proposition you. In front of m... all of us. She was *naked*," Keely says, exasperated. "I mean, seriously?"

"I saw that." This time I smirk.

"Perv."

"I'm a red-blooded male. Can you blame me? The woman I wanted, no, *want* in my bed was ghosting me. I had every right to take advantage of that opportunity."

Keely is looking everywhere but at me.

"Keely?"

"Look." Keely stands and moves to the furthest part of my living room. I watch as she picks up little things I've got sitting on my shelves, like my badge from Phoenix P.D. and a small plaque recognizing me for developing the school safety program from the same city. "I can't be with you."

"Why not?"

"I hate cops."

"So you've said. Why do you hate cops?" It'd better not be because one of them hurt her. I'll need names if that's the case. Someone's getting an ass-kicking right before I turn them in to the captain.

She stops touching things and stares at me. Our eyes meet. "I can't tell you the entire story. It's not about me. But hopefully this will help you understand why I just... can't with you."

I nod and wait.

Keely moves to sit in the chair directly across from me. The coffee table separates us. She leans forward until her elbows are on her knees.

"Someone I love was assaulted."

"Okay." I lean forward too.

"She didn't tell anyone for a week. Not until I showed up. When she told me, I talked her into going to the police."

"Was this in Page?"

"No. It was in another city."

"Phoenix?"

"Nick? Are you going to let me speak?"

"Sure. Sorry."

"Not in Phoenix either. It doesn't matter where."

The hell it doesn't.

"We went to the police and they did nothing. Worse than nothing. They told her she'd waited too long, that it was her word against his, and no one would believe her." Keely's face has turned from pink to flushed red as she tells her story. "He..." she pauses. "One of those assholes had the gall to tell her it was her fault for going to the party in the first place."

I watch as a tear runs down her sweet face.

"You're fucking kidding me!" I'm up out of my chair and stomping to the door and back. "That did not happen!" I say it so loudly it echoes off the walls.

Her head rears back. "You don't believe me? Well, fuck you, Nick." She's now up and making her way toward the front door.

"No." I stop her before she can rush out. "I believe you. One hundred percent I believe you. I was just reacting. No, I know there are cops who don't deserve to wear the badge. Who was the cop? When was this? Where did it happen? Hell. Who assaulted her?" I bet he's done it before or again. Those fuckers always repeat.

"Nick. I—"

I slide my hands down her arms to her wrists. "Tell me."

"There's nothing you can do. It was years ago."

"I can do something."

"It's too late."

"Was it less than seven years ago?"

"Almost. A little over six years ago."

"Then there's still time."

"No. Nick. She doesn't want to go through that again. It's too hard for her. She's always been an introvert, but that thing with that asshole nearly killed her. She used to be more... I don't know—vibrant. Now she's so"—Keely places her palm over her chest, over her heart—"withdrawn."

"Keely. He's probably done it to others."

Keely looks at me, blinking. A lone tear slides down her cheek. "That's not Violet's fault."

"Your sister?"

"Shit." She gives her own forehead a head slap. "I didn't mean to tell you that but yes, my twin. And it's that fucking cop's fault. He did nothing. We even tried to go over his head but that was worse than useless. We were 'escorted' out by a younger cop after the asshole in charge refused to listen. When we got to the front door of the station, he stopped us."

"He stopped you?"

Keely nodded her head. "He put his hand on her arm to stop her from leaving so he could mock her. The fucking asshole m-mocked her, Nick."

Keely is crying big wet tears now. Her little body is shaking so hard. I pull her against me and, thankfully, she lets me. "Baby," I whisper.

"H-he told her sh-she should be lucky someone paid that kind of attention to her."

Fuck! I want to scream. I want to kill some fucking cops. "Where was this? What city?"

"Tucson. But I don't want you to do anything. She's been doing the work to get back on track. She's been going out with us. She's taking care of herself. I think she's learning self-defense."

I nod, but my mind is all over the place. "Still—"

"No, Nick. I have to think about what Vi wants."

"Are you sure that's what she wants? Have you asked her? Talked to her about it recently?"

"No. Not for a long time."

I place my hand on her cheek wiping away wetness with my thumb. "Talk to her. If you get her okay, I'll do some checking. Do you have the original police report?"

"She does, I think."

Taking hold of her hand, I move to the sofa and pull her into my lap. I place one palm on the knee furthest from me and my other on her lower back. Rubbing that up and down, I say evenly, "I can see why you hate cops, baby girl, but not all of us are scum of the earth like those guys. I've got your back on this." *On everything.* "If you want me to do it, I'll investigate. But time is of the essence."

Keely leans her head down until it's on my shoulder. With a deep sigh, she says, "It's been hard holding all that anger in, Nick. But, honest to God, I wanted to kill those cops. My sister was a lot bigger back then. She's tall anyway, but she'd gained the freshman thirty. And that was on top of high school weight. So she was self-conscious. They just dug the knife in deeper like the fucking assault wasn't enough."

I feel her wipe her nose on my shoulder and I don't give a shit. Wrapping her up tightly in my arms, I lean back and pull her further into my lap. As quiet as I can, I say, "I'm not them, Keely."

"Aren't you?"

"No. I'm nothing like that. If you give me a shot, I'll show you."

"I can't."

Why the fuck not? Goddamn this girl is making me crazy. But I stay calm. "Why not?"

"Because I promised Violet."

"You promised her what?" I know what she's going to say.

"That I'd hate cops forever."

"Did Violet promise the same?"

Keely scoffs and wipes her face with the back of her hands. "Violet's too kindhearted. I told her I'd do it for both of us."

Interesting. "Has she had therapy?" I always recommend that to survivors no matter how they were treated by the police.

"She had counseling, yes. Right after."

"Maybe you should talk to her? See if she'll let me do a little digging. At least I could check on that fucker who attacked her."

Keely pulls away, attempting to slide off my lap. "No, Nick. She was terrified of that guy. He was BMOC."

I furrow my brows. "What's that?"

"Big Man on Campus. He was king shit. She dropped out of school in the middle of the semester and moved home just so she'd never have to see him again."

Pulling her back against me, I lean in and kiss her neck. "I swear to you, I'll be discreet."

She moves her head so I can kiss her right below her ear. "I barely know you."

"I want a shot with you. Let me do some checking. Trust me."

"I don't trust you. But...."

I use my palm to nudge her face until she's looking into my eyes. "But?"

"I'll ask Violet if I can give you his name. It's up to her."

I nod and kiss her lips softly. "That's a start." I'll take what I can get. I want a beginning.

CHAPTER EIGHTEEN

KEELY

I CAN'T BELIEVE I'm doing this. No, not the kissing part. I'm all in on that. No, I can't believe I'm even considering letting him look into Violet's assault.

I need to talk to her.

"You need to get out of your own head, babe. Stop thinking about that. Think about this." Nick reaches up, sliding his palm over my breast and pinching my nipple through my clothes. I moan and arch my back like a feline. The next thing I know, he's got the top of my favorite off-the-shoulder dress pushed down to my waist. The guy doesn't waste time.

"No bra?" His palm is skimming over my nipples lightly. He's teasing me. "Naughty girl." Nick's voice is deeper than usual. Husky.

"The d-dress has a shelf bra." I hate bras, so if I see an opportunity to go without, I take it.

Pinching my nipple again, I watch as Nick lowers his head

and swipes my left breast with his tongue. I lean in so he'll do it again. He doesn't. This time, he opens his mouth and takes as much of me as he can inside, suckling me. I begin to pant; it's turning me on so much I'm starting to wiggle my ass. Sliding a free hand into his hair, I pull him in closer. "More."

Without a word, Nick lifts me until I'm straddling him. This is familiar. He immediately begins work on the other breast. I'd love to push him back and do things to him, but I swear I'm about to come from his mouth alone. "Nick. Please," I whine.

Pulling back, Nick slides his palms beneath my skirt. When I look down, I watch him unbuckle his belt and then unzip his pants. "Scoot off for a second, babe."

I slide off his lap and stare down. His hips rise, bringing his tent closer to me. Nick pushes his pants and boxers down until his cock pops free. "Jesus." He's got a pretty dick.

In seconds, his bottoms are on the floor somewhere and I'm still staring down at his dick. Licking my lips, I quickly glance at him before leaning down for a taste. I swipe my tongue over his head and moan. Something you should probably know about me? I like oral. Giving and receiving. I especially like to drive the guy nuts with my mouth. They're at my mercy, and that's empowering, ladies, trust me.

I slowly lick up his shaft from the base to the head. My tongue is stiff enough to put pressure on the vein there. At the head, I lick around and around, then slide my mouth over it and suck.

"Jesus fucking Christ," Nick yelps, his hips thrusting upwards.

See what I mean?

I look up at his face and smirk. Okay, his dick is in my mouth, so I'm attempting a smirk. I repeat my first set of moves, then I grasp his cock at the base and pump him up and down as I suck.

"Keely." Nick's breathless. "Stop."

I pause to look up at him. "Why?"

"I want you. If you keep that up, I'll come too soon."

"Fine." I move to stand. "Where's your bedroom?"

Nick stands, his dick still hard as nails. Taking my hand in his, he leads me down the hallway. When we walk into his room, I stop.

"This is nice." The room is understated, with medium gray walls and some black-and-white landscape images hanging above the bed. There's matching dark furniture and a huge bed covered in crisp white linens. It's simple and masculine.

"Thanks."

I push my dress off the rest of the way, leaving me in lacy white boy shorts. Turning to face him, I see Nick taking off his shirt, and I get a look at his naked ass. It's better than I thought it'd be. Seeing his buns through his boxers during life drawing is nothing compared to the real thing. His butt is firm and muscled, plus he's got those two little dimples right above each cheek. I want to lick those.

"Lie on the bed, Keely."

I hadn't realized he was approaching me. I step backwards to his bed and sit. Scooting up to the middle, I lift my hips in an effort to slide my undies off. I lie back but prop myself up with my elbows.

"You on birth control, Keely?"

"Yes." I know where this is going.

Reaching into his nightstand, Nick pulls out a piece of paper, laying it gently on my stomach. "I'm clean. Just had a physical and blood workup as a requirement of the job."

I lift the paper and read. Nicholas Bernard Martelli is indeed clean. Not only that, he's six feet two, 185 pounds, and has only a 7 percent body mass index. Damn. I've got 7 percent body fat too. On my left foot.

I read on. He's up-to-date on his immunizations, he doesn't take any daily medications, he suffers from seasonal allergies, and he apparently needs glasses. "You wear glasses?"

"Contacts, but I took them out." He reaches into his nightstand and pulls out some specs.

The second he slides them on, I smile. Big. "Hot as hell, Nick."

"Yeah?"

"Hell, yeah. Will you wear them for me while we fuck?"

"Seriously?" He appears to be surprised.

"Absolutely." I reach out to run my palm over his still-hard cock.

"You done?" Nick nods to the paper in my hand.

I flip it over to the section about blood and read his results. He's clean. "Do you go bareback often?"

"Never, actually." Nick's moved up onto the bed and is now on his knees between my legs.

"I'm confused."

His palms start at my ankles and slowly move up my calves. "About?"

"You want to fuck me bare?"

"Yes. Badly."

Now his big palms move inward from the top of my thighs. I spread my legs wider to make room for whatever it is he's about to do.

"We haven't talked... oh, shit." Nick's mouth is right where I want it. His tongue is everywhere. His face and eyes are intense, focused.

"Talked? About this?" Nick raises his hand and points to me, then to himself.

"Yes." Shit. He's moving away. Going in the wrong direction. Backing up until he's sitting on his haunches.

"What are we doing here, Keely?"

It's hard to concentrate. His dick is still thick and hard. How can he sustain that?

"Keely." It's a statement, not a question. "What are we doing?"

The hell if I know. "Fucking?" I shrug for emphasis.

"Fucking." He releases a deep breath as he runs a hand through his hair. "Is that all this is to you?"

What does he expect me to say here? We practically just met. I don't know him well enough to assess whether or not this is more than a fuck-buddy arrangement. I should just say that—be honest. "I don't know you well enough to assess what this is."

"Do you want to get to know me?"

I swear he's looking at me like I'm about to deliver bad news. "Nick. I...."

He pushes off the bed, picking up his boxers. I watch him slide them up his legs and over his now only semihard dick. Next, he opens a drawer and pulls out a T-shirt. It's navy blue and, from what I can see so far, it's tight in all the right places.

"What are you doing?" I say, still lying naked on his bed.

"We're going to get to know each other."

"Now?" I squeak.

"Now."

I quickly move off the bed in search of my dress. Finding it in a heap near the bed, I slide it up over my hips, then pull it up to cover me. I spy my underwear hanging off the end of the bed, so I reach for them and slip them on.

The entire time I'm dressing, I'm also fuming. I can't with this guy. I just can't. He's so damn bossy. He left me without an orgasm so we could "talk." During sex. No. So *he* could talk. Sure, I wanted to talk but I was thinking *after*. Well, I've got a big surprise for him.

I march out into the living room, Nick follows close behind.

My shoes are next to the sofa, so I slide those on. Reaching out, I pick up my small clutch purse and move to the door.

"Where are you going, Keely?" His voice sounds tired. Resigned.

"I'm leaving. Thanks for..." I look out into his living room looking for something to thank him for. "The wine."

"Keely. Come on."

Pulling open the door, I stop and turn to him. "Nick. This is all going too fast. You're pushing me into something I can't wrap my head around."

"Okay." He steps closer. "If we're going too fast and you can't wrap your head around it, what can I do to help you with that?"

"Slow down. Give me room to breathe. I meant what I said about cops. I get that you think you're different. Maybe I can see that, maybe I can't. But if you're looking for something long-term here," I point to him then at me, "I can't. I had fun fucking you. I liked having you as my dirty secret." Although now that Michael, Sally, Julia, and Kimberly know, that's no longer true. Everyone will know soon enough. "It's too much too soon."

"I can slow down."

I roll my eyes and look up and away from him. "Why?"

"Why, what?"

I shrug. "I'm nothing special." There are days when I ooze confidence outwardly, but I know, inside, I'm just like everyone else.

Nick's face gets angry all of a sudden. "Keely. I don't want to hear negative shit like that from you. You're very special."

I snort, because who wouldn't?

"You're smart and beautiful; you care for your friends and family deeply. And your students. What about them?"

"What about them?"

"I *know* they love you. How could they not?"

They do. They love me as much as I adore them.

He keeps listing off things he thinks make me special. "You make me laugh, you're amazing in the sack."

Eye roll again. "I know."

"Your body is rockin'. I want to be with you all the time. I can't stop thinking about you."

"You can't?"

"I can't. I've wanted to text you every hour, every day since we started talking."

"That's sort of sweet. Stalkery, but sweet."

"I'm not sweet, babe. But I could be for you."

"Listen, Nick." I take one step closer to him. "I can't do anything until I talk to Violet."

He starts to say something.

"And before you ask me when I'm doing that, the answer is, I don't know."

"Fine." Both of his hands move up to rub his ruggedly handsome face. "I can wait."

"You can?" I look down at his boxers. He's still pretty much erect.

"I can. I've got a hand, don't I?" He chuckles.

"You'd rather wait until I figure shit out? We could be screwing like rabbits in secret right now. Like seriously, right this minute." Hell, I would have orgasmed by now probably.

Nick's arms are around me in a flash, pulling me into him. I feel him against my stomach. "I don't want to be secret with you. I want to take you out, be seen with you in public. I want to meet your sisters, your dad. I want it all."

It's my turn to rub my face. I don't get it. No guy has ever wanted anything close to that with me. Sure, I've had boyfriends here and there, like the one in high school I thought was my one true love, and the other in college that could have made the cut if he hadn't fucked my roommate behind my back.

"I need to think. I need time."

"I can give you that." He leans in to me and kisses my lips softly. "I'd like to call you and text, if that's okay."

"Sure. You're saved as Olivia Benson on my phone."

He looks confused. Time to clarify.

"*Law and Order: SVU*. She's the lead character."

He still looks perplexed.

"She's a cop." I pause. "On TV."

He starts to chuckle, resting his forehead on mine. "Just screwing with you, clever girl. Love that show." Kissing me one more time, he taps my nose with his finger.

He's right about one thing. I'm clever A.F.

CHAPTER NINETEEN

Nick

IT'S BEEN ALMOST two weeks since Keely was at my place. In that time, the only contact we've had has been via text messages and the one time I saw her, at Murphy's Pub about a week ago. Even then I merely waved, because she was with her sisters. It was the first glimpse I'd gotten of all of them. There were a couple guys with them too, but none of them seemed to be with her. Thankfully.

Keeton Gustafson was there. His arm was around the only brunette in the group. Another tall, older guy was there with a woman with strawberry blonde hair. A tall redhead sat beside Keely, and I wondered if that was Violet. She was definitely taller than the other sisters, but I couldn't be sure since there was one other woman at the table. No, the tall one has to be Violet, because I've met Sadie at her bakery, Sadie Cakes, a number of times. And before you make a joke about cops and donuts, just know I like cupcakes too. Oh, and Danish. And pie. Don't forget about pie. The coffee isn't bad either.

I made a mental note that Keely was the only true blonde in the family, not that it matters. Just an observation.

When she saw me at the bar, she smiled, gave me a nod, and turned back to the group. Later that night, I sat in my bed, holding my phone, hoping she'd call or text. I gave up waiting at about midnight, deciding to send her something myself.

Me: You make it home safe and sound?
Keely: Yeppers. Home and sleepy-weepy.
Me: And drunk?
Keely: Drunky wunky.

Definitely drunk.

Keely: I wish you were here.

Oh, shit. Drunk Keely is not who I want to be with, necessarily.

Me: Me too.
Keely: Come over.
Me: Is this a booty call or something more.

Because I want more.

Keely: ...
Me: Keely?

I didn't hear another word from her that night.
She was sticking to her guns, damn it. I suppose being true

to your word is a good quality to have, but not when it comes to me and Keely. I want her to finally see what *I* see and give in to it. Hell, everything about our relationship, if you can call it that, is good. Even text messaging. I'm not referring to sexting, but I bet she'd be talented in that arena as well. No, just text message banter. For example, the one I sent her the same night she left my apartment two weeks ago.

Me: Do you miss me?
Keely: Who is this?
Me: Smart ass.
Keely: Better than a dumb ass ;)

I laughed off and on the rest of the night after that little exchange. The next day, she sent me a photo of the lacy edge of her panties with just a glimpse of porcelain skin. Alright, I know, I said we weren't sexting. We haven't been. But I don't count a sexy message as sexting. It was hot nonetheless.

The next day, she sent me this:

Keely: Let's play a game
Me: Okay. What kind of game?
Keely: Sort of like 20 questions
Me: Got it.
Keely: Ready?
Me: Ready
Keely: Favorite color
Me: Black
Keely: Favorite food

She's playing the "get to know you" game. Interesting.

Me: Lasagna. No wait. Pizza
Keely: Favorite position
Me: I assume you mean sexual position. On the bottom
Keely: Okay, favorite movie
Me: *Slap Shot* (the old one)
Keely: Never heard of it. Fav TV show
Me: *Game of Thrones*
Keely: Ooh, me too. We should watch it sometime
Me: Anytime
Keely: Republican or Democrat?

Tough one. I could get into trouble here.

Me: Independent
Keely: LOL. Very diplomatic of you
Keely: Religious?
Me: Catholic. Non-practicing
Me: My turn. Favorite color?
Keely: I'll save you time. Here are my answers in the same order: Yellow, buffalo wings from Murphy's but Giovanni's lasagna is a close second, like we did it or cowgirl.

Sweet Jesus. We did it with her on her hands and knees. Fuck, that was hot.

Keely: *Pride and Prejudice*. The old one.
Me: Really?
Keely: It was one of my mom's favorites. She thought Colin Firth was hot stuff.
Me: That's cool. I've never seen it, but I'd watch it with you if you want

Keely: That'd be cool. Thanks

Keely: Okay, let me finish up my list... *Game of Thrones*, neither. I hate politics. No religious affiliation but I consider myself spiritual.

Me: I liked playing that game. I got to know more about you.

Keely: Me too. Tomorrow we can play again. I've got more questions.

Me: You can come over and ask me in person.

Keely: Nah. We'll text. Night.

Me: Night.

It was worth a try.

I waited for her to text the next evening, but I got nothing. Actually, I had to wait three more days for her next round of questions. Now, if you think I need to be taking more of a lead here, I agree. However, I told her I'd give her space and time, and that's what I'm doing. If she contacts me, I'll go from there.

Finally, on day four she wrote:

Keely: Favorite music.

Me: Country, Rock-n-Roll, Blues, R&B. You?

Keely: Elvis Costello. How old were you when you lost your virginity?

Me: I like E.C. 15. You?

Keely: Barely out of diapers, young man. I was 17.

Keely: Romantic or Pragmatist

Me: Both. You?

Keely: Both. Gun control or no?

Me: Common sense gun policies. I'm a big advocate for requiring gun training and lessons. Like we do before you can drive a car.

Keely: Hm, okay. That could work. I don't like the idea of people carrying guns in school. I wouldn't trust Michael to not shoot me instead of a perp.

Me: A perp? You a cop now?

Keely: LOL. No, my sister Agatha fancies herself a detective of sorts. She's rubbing off on me. Okay. Next question… if you could be any animal, which would you be and why?

That's a tough one…

Me: Eagle. Because they're fucking majestic.

Keely: My sister's house cat. He's spoiled rotten and gets to sleep all day.

Me: Maybe I should change mine. We could sleep together.

Keely: Ha! Good one. Halloween or Christmas?

Me: Christmas. You?

Keely: Halloween. 100%. Love to dress up. Okay, last one for tonight. If there was a fire, what would you save? Not people or pets. Assume they're safe.

Me: The picture of my mom on my shelf.

Keely: Me too.

I didn't hear anything else that night. What was there to say after that last question? It bummed me out, so I know it made her feel the same.

The next night:

Keely: Ready for more?

Me: Absolutely. Fire away.

Keely: On a scale of 1-10, how cool are you? I'm a 10 in case you were curious.

Me: I know you're a 10, babe. I'd say 7.5 for me.

Keely: Which celebrity would you sleep with if you had a hall pass?

Me: Jennifer Lawrence. You?

Keely: She's hot. I'd do her. Mine? Jason Momoa. Ooh, or Jacob Elordi. <3 <3

Me: I know of Momoa, not Elordi, but I can't think straight now that I'm picturing you and J-Law together.

Keely: Perv. Elordi's hot. You should check him out. LOL

Keely: Describe the perfect kiss in three words.

Me: Keely May Palmer.

Keely: Ooh, well played, old man. Well played. What superpower would you have if you were a superhero?

I'm going to let the "old" comment go for now.

Me: Invisibility. I could catch all sorts of criminals. You didn't describe your perfect kiss yet.

Keely: True. My superpower would be healing.

I get why. Her mom.

Keely: The kiss? Unexpected, intimate, ardent.

Me: Good one.

Keely: Sweet or savory?

Me: Sweet. You?

Keely: Same. My sister, the baker, would kill me if I didn't have the Palmer sweet tooth. Ha! Okay. Last one.

I hope she just means for the night.

Keely: Dr. Who or Star Trek?

Me: That's a hard one.

Keely: That's what she said. **Snort**

Me: **eye roll** Probably Dr. Who, but I think I prefer Red Dwarf.

Keely: OMG! I love that show. Read the books. They're hilarious. Time for bed. Night, Nick.

Me: I will check them out. Night, babe.

SO, here I sit again, in my bed, holding my phone in the hopes she sends me a text or, better yet, calls me. I haven't heard her voice. While I've enjoyed the questions and the back and forth, I want to talk to her. Hell, I want to touch her. Fuck it, I'll initiate.

Me: You awake?

I only have to wait a minute or two.

Keely: It's nine at night. Of course I'm awake. I'm not a grandma.

I chuckle at her response.

Me: Well, then. You should come over.

Keely: ...

Me: Are you thinking about it?

Please fucking say yes.

Keely: No. I'm working on my bug unit for my class.

Me: Oh? What does that entail?

Keely: Well, we've been studying bugs for several weeks. We've done an art project; we've listened to bug music and sounds.

Me: Bug music?

Keely: It's a thing. I swear. Anyway, we've learned the biology of insects, their parts, etc.

Me: Wow, this is a very comprehensive bug unit.

Keely: It's part of our curriculum. We're finishing it up next week with a visit to old Mrs. Silver's butterfly garden.

Me: I've never met her.

Keely: She knows my dad. She's a nice lady, doesn't even bitch when the kids trample her vegetable garden when we visit every spring. LOL.

Me: Would you like police protection during your outing?

Keely: You mean another adult chaperone? Hell yes. Those little buggers take off on me all the time.

Me: Great. Tell me when and where. I'll be there.

Keely: Next Tuesday. We'll leave at 10:00. Mrs. Silver's house is only a block away.

Me: Can't wait.

No lie. I can't wait to see her with her "little beans."

CHAPTER TWENTY

KEELY

"OKAY, munchkins. It's time to line up. Where's my line leader?" I look around the room. It's bedlam. I let them choose a center to work in this morning until we head out for Mrs. Silver's place. Michael's doing the same thing in his room, since his kiddos are doing the insect unit too. I look for Callie Smart, today's line leader, and spot her over in the craft center. She's always there. Not a surprise since her mom, Becca Smart, is our art teacher. "Callie? Get a move on, line leader."

The minute she hears her name, she looks up. I ask her again, "Aren't you my line leader?"

"Yes," she says softly. The girl is shy, that's for sure. She'd give Violet a run for her money.

"Well then, come on."

She puts her crayons away and walks quickly to the door.

"Now, the rest of you line up, please."

I watch as almost all of them leave what they're doing to line up. Everyone but Henry. He'd rather stay in the reading corner than go anywhere outside.

"Henry, time to go."

Setting his book down, he stands up and walks slowly to the line, shoulders slumped. Patting his shoulder, I say, "You'll get to read again this afternoon. Okay?"

"Okay, Miss Palmer." My goodness, he sounds so pitiful.

I've made my way to the front of the line to open the door when a knock sounds. I've got a small window in my door and see Officer Nick Martelli—at least part of him—in the window.

I thought he was meeting us at Mrs. Silver's. I guess I wasn't clear on that. I told him the day and time we were leaving.

Suddenly, I'm as nervous as a whore in church. Okay, it's not that bad, but I'm pretty damn nervous.

I turn to my kiddos. "Stay put. I'll be two minutes."

Opening the door, I look up at a smiling Officer Nick Martelli in his full uniform. "Are you on duty?"

"I am, but I have permission to escort your group to the butterfly garden. Community outreach." He smirks.

"Is that what you're calling it?" I snicker.

"No. It's what Captain Morgan called it."

Michael's door opens into the hallway, and Nick and I both turn to watch him lead his group out. "You ready?" he says, smiling. It's fake. He hates field trips. The kids go nutso outside.

"Ready."

"Ooh, Officer Martelli," Michael coos. "Are you going with us?"

"Community outreach."

"Is that what they're calling it?" he says with a giggle.

"Yes," Nick deadpans.

"Okaa-aay," Michael sings. "Let's go. It's going to be hotter than a witch's you-know-what in an hour."

Pulling the door open, I'm shocked to see the kids are still in line. By the looks on their faces, they're too intrigued by the police officer at the door to do anything else.

"Beans, this is Officer Martelli. Can you say hello?"

All together, they say, "Hello, Officer Martelli." They say it so slow—it's hilarious.

"Hi, kids. Mind if I go with you to see the butterflies?"

"No," they all say at once.

Then Augustus, my precious little terror, asks, "Hey, mister. Can I play with your gun?"

"No." Nick doesn't even try to sugarcoat it.

"Okay, then." I clap my hands. "Let's move out. Mr. Brook's class is already walking."

Mrs. Silver only lives about a block away from the school, but we have to cross two streets to get there. I ask Nick to take the rear and make sure they're all holding hands. It's adorable when they do that. They look like little ducklings crossing the street.

Once we're safely at Mrs. Silver's, we move over to stand with Michael's group as Mrs. Silver talks about her butterfly garden, the flowers she plants to attract them, and the kinds of butterflies that are indigenous to northern Arizona.

"The monarch butterfly is the one I see the most," she explains.

Just then, one of them flutters over to her face and sits on her nose. The kids erupt into laughter at the sight. Mrs. S. plays it up well. Her eyes grow huge and round like she's in shock. But she recovers quickly. "Oh, I recognize this little fella. His name is Albert."

The kids lose it again. I see Nick from the corner of my eye chuckling too. When he turns his head, our eyes meet. He gives me the smile to end all smiles. He's having fun. So am I.

We spend forty-five minutes at Mrs. Silver's place. Just the right amount of time for active kindergartners. Michael and I gather our kids up so we can walk separately. My class heads out first. It'll be lunch time when we get back, then recess. That means they'll be good and tired this afternoon. That's the best time to read stories.

"Nick. You don't have to walk us back."

"I know. I want to." He pauses. "Community outreach."

"You can have lunch with me. It's taco Tuesday. Yummy."

"School lunch?"

"Sure. It's not terrible." I snicker. "It's not that great either."

"I'd love to, Keely."

"Mister," Henry says, tugging on Nick's leg.

"Yes?" he says, looking down at Henry.

"Her name is Miss Palmer. Not Keeeeeely. It's impropriate to call her that."

"Right." Nick looks up at me. "I'm sorry, Miss Palmer. I didn't mean to be *im*propriate."

"Thank you, Officer Martelli."

Nick moves to the back of the line as we approach our first street crossing. There's something really domestic about him being here.

At the front door of the school, I wait for all of the kiddos to catch up.

"Remember," I place my finger over my lips, "we need to *beeeee* quiet in the hallway. Get it? Bee? Insects?" God, I'm good.

With everyone quiet, I open the door and walk through. I ask the second student in line, Henry, to hold the door for every-one. "Catch up after everyone is through the door, Henry." These little people don't like to lose their place in line. I get that. It's how they roll. I peek back at Officer Hottie at the back and see that Augustus is chattering away at him. Probably asking him if he can see his gun again.

As I pass the office, I look in the window to wave, but no one is about. Strange. Continuing on, we pass the music room. I pause and wait for the kids, because I tend to walk fast. From here, I can see Michael's group has caught up to us. I'm about to continue on when I hear someone shouting. It's a man, and he's loud. I turn back to my kids. Leave it to Henry to notice, "*That guy isn't quiet in the hallway.*"

"No," I laugh. "He's—"

I'm stopped midsentence by a loud popping sound. More than one. I look back at the end of the line and watch, like it's in slow motion, as Nick draws his weapon. "Nick?"

He runs to me. Not a jog. He runs. When he reaches me, he moves to stand between me and whatever the popping sound was.

"Keely. Listen to me. I need you to move into that room," he points to the music room. "Walk through and out the door. I need all of you to keep moving once you're outside. Crouch down and move as fast as you can. Get back to Mrs. Silver's. I'll come for you there."

"Nick? What's going—"

Three more pops sound, louder than before.

"Move, Keely. Now," Nick says in a quiet but demanding voice. Then he adds, "You've got this, baby. Just stay calm and get out of here as fast as you can."

I quickly turn to my kids. "Hey, guess what? We're having a picnic outside. Follow me. Hurry, little beans, last one out is a rotten egg." I walk into the empty music room and hold the door for my kids and Michael's. He's at the end of the line. I'm surprised how fast everyone has moved. Once Michael is through the door, I turn back and see Nick racing down the hallway with his gun out. He's running to whatever is going on. I hear two more popping sounds as Michael grabs me by the arm and yanks me out the back door. "Move, Keely. Move. Move. Move."

"Are those shots?"

"Yes. Move, girl. Let's get us all to safety."

I race out the door and do as Nick asks. I crouch low and direct the kids to do the same. We move along the brick exterior in the direction of the front of the building. I don't know what to do once we get to the parking lot.

I look to Michael. "Keep going. Let's get back to Mrs. Silver's just like Nick said."

"Good. Yeah. Good."

"Let's go, kids. Mrs. Silver has ice cream!"

"Yeah!" they all yell.

The sirens sound off in the distance before we've reached the first cross street. So many sirens.

"Miss Palmer! Miss Palmer! Fire trucks!" one of the kiddos yells.

"I know. It's just a drill. Let's keep going before the ice cream melts." Shit. I feel terrible lying to them, but it can't be helped.

Thank goodness they have no idea what was going on back there.

CHAPTER TWENTY-ONE

Nick

THE INSTANT I heard the first shot, I pulled my weapon and ran to Keely. I've been trained to deal with this shit, but I haven't had to handle a situation where someone I care about is in the cross fire, literally.

As I act as cover so Michael and Keely can get the kids into the room, I flip on my radio to alert dispatch and turn down the radio just low enough for me to hear any responses. "This is echo nine seven. Ten-seventy-one in progress. Shots fired. Page Elementary School. 1300 South Navajo. Need backup. Copy."

"Copy that. Attention all units. Ten-seventy-one in progress. 1300 South Navajo. Need backup. Copy."

Before I take off, I look into the room and see Michael and Keely begin to push through the outside door. That's when I make my move. Holding my firearm to my side, I run as fast as I can to the gunfire. The sooner I'm there, the sooner this fucker is down.

I begin to hear sirens off in the distance. My brothers and sisters are on the way. Now, hopefully, I can get this fucker before anyone else gets hurt.

Sliding my back against the wall, I approach a hallway that turns to my right. Raising my gun to my shoulder, I look around the bend and see one body. A woman. And too much blood. I can't tell from here if she's alive or dead. I can assess that as soon as I take this guy out. Looking further down the hallway, I see him about thirty feet from me. He's standing, alone, with the gun at his side. The only good thing about this situation is he's no longer shooting, but he's still armed.

Stepping out into the hallway, I shout, "Freeze. Police."

I must have surprised the asshole, because the first thing he does is raise his gun, aiming it right at me. I shoot three times. I hit him in the chest, shoulder, and thigh. As he falls to the ground, he releases the weapon, the gun making a clinking sound as it hits the hard tile floor. It's still close enough to his hand for him to reach it, so holding my gun steady, I move deliberately toward him. He's blinking; he's still alive. As soon as I get close enough, I kick the gun away.

He begins to speak in a raspy voice. "She was taking my baby away from me".

I move behind him, checking his person for any additional weapons. Once I know he's got no other firearms, I press the button on my shoulder radio. "Ten-twenty-six. Subject down."

"Th-that b-bitch was t-taking my daughter." His voice sounds hoarse. "Fuck. It hurts."

Looking over at the woman on the floor, I know I need to move to her quickly. As I'm about to secure this asshole's hands, I hear pounding footsteps. My backup.

From there, it's like a well-choreographed war zone. Cops and paramedics move through each room, searching for the injured or worse. Several people are taken out on gurneys, including the suspect. He's still alive. Sadly, one person is not. She's in a body bag.

CHAPTER TWENTY-TWO

KEELY

WE GET to Mrs. Silver's in half the time as before. I rush to the door and knock frantically. When she answers, I lean in and whisper in her ear. I swear her face turns white as snow.

The sirens are screaming louder and louder as they get closer. I hope they're in time. I hope Nick was in time.

"Ice cream!" shouts one of Michael's kids.

Mrs. Silver's eyes get huge. "I've got cookies."

A fire truck and an ambulance speed past Mrs. Silver's place.

"Fire truck!" one of the kids yells excitedly.

"Abuwance!" shouts another.

"Cookies!" bellows someone else.

Looking at the sweet older woman, I whisper just loud enough for her to hear, "Thank you."

Several other emergency vehicles whip past her house, sirens blasting, as we walk around the house to her back garden.

Once the kids are seated in her backyard, I pull out my phone from my back pocket and stare at it. I want to text Nick—find out if he's okay.

Shit. Nick. He just ran right into danger.

Then I think about my teacher friends. My besties. *Oh, God.* I look over at Michael. I know I look terrified. Hot tears start to form in the corners of my eyes.

"Michael. What about Sally? Kimberly? Julia?"

"I know, sweetie. We'll know more soon. I've sent texts to all three of them and Pam." Our principal. "You need to call your dad."

Oh, shit. I'm sure he's heard about this by now. I decide to text him. My voice is going to give me away.

Me: Dad. I'm okay. I can't talk right now. Got my students to Mrs. Silver's house. Tell the girls. More later.
Dad: Thank God. I'll call your sisters.

I should text Nick, but I decide to wait.

Placing my phone next to my hip, I look at my students. They're oblivious, thankfully. It's getting hot outside, but they don't seem to care. Michael, the cool and collected one of our pair, has started playing a game with them. Leapfrog. I want to smile. I try, but I can't. The best I can do is will back the tears that are begging to get out.

I stand to watch the kids play, clapping every once in a while to make it look like I'm having fun, but really all I'm doing is looking out to the street for a gorgeous man in black to approach. He told me he'd find us here. I believe him.

IT FEELS like it's been hours at Mrs. Silver's house, but in reality, it's only been about an hour. I've been craning my head so often, looking for Nick to walk around the corner, that when he does, I think it's a mirage. Not for long, though, because the second I realize he's real, I run. I run so fast I nearly trip on my way to him.

"Nick!" I shout several times along the way. As soon as I'm close enough, I launch myself at him. With my arms around his neck and my legs around his waist, I start to kiss him all over his pretty face while saying things I've been thinking for the last hour. "Thank God. I was so worried." I kiss his cheek, eyelids, his ear. "I was so s-scared." I begin to cry then. All those tears I was holding on to for this entire episode.

"Shh, baby," he whispers. "I've got you."

I stop kissing him because there are little children who're asking a lot of questions behind me right now. Sliding down his body, I land on my feet. Wiping away the tears, I look at him. "Nick?"

"Later," he whispers. "We need to get them back. Parents have started to arrive. They want their kids."

I bet they do. Getting myself together, I rotate to face the kids. "Time to go back to school."

"No...," several of them grumble.

I want to laugh, but I can't. Not yet. Maybe not ever again.

Nick takes the back of the line, Michael the middle, and I lead us all back to school. The second we're on school grounds, some of the parents who are waiting back near a taped-off area glimpse us and start to run toward us. I recognize several of my kids' parents right away. Many of them are crying or look as though they've been crying.

One of them thanks me. "Thank you for getting them to safety, Keely."

I nod, not knowing what to say or even who said it. "I'm just glad they're safe."

I feel a hand on my hip and a breath on my ear. "Who is Callie?"

I blink at his words. "Callie Smart?"

"Yes."

Oh, no. Oh no. "W-why?"

"Keely," he says softly. "Baby, which one is Callie? I need her to come with me."

I walk numbly over to the little ginger-headed angel from my class. My artist. Kneeling down in front of her, I smile as I push a stray curl away from her pretty little face. "Callie? Officer Martelli wants to talk to you. Okay?"

"W-will you go with me?"

"I sure will."

Holding her hand, I take her to Nick. He squats in front of her. "Callie? I need to take you to visit with the principal. Your aunt is on her way to get you."

I look into Nick's eyes and see sadness. My heart flops over in my chest. This isn't good. Not at all.

"Where's Mommy?"

He doesn't answer; he merely gives her a warm smile. "Your aunt wants to see you."

"Okay." Callie's voice is soft. So soft I barely made out the words.

"Keely!" shouts someone to my left. Sally is running toward me. I want to run to her, but I can't leave Callie right now. When she gets to me, she wraps me up in her arms. "Shh. Callie."

"I know." Sally is sobbing in my ear. Pulling out of her arms, I look down at Callie, then at Nick.

"Let me walk her." Together, Nick and I each take one of Callie's hands and lead her to Principal Pam.

A large group of our faculty and staff are standing together near the front entrance of the school. When we get close enough, all eyes turn to Callie. Several sobs erupt, but I ignore them, because if I don't, I'm going to lose it too. Pam steps out of the group and moves to Callie quickly. "Aunt Val is coming to get you, honey. She's anxious to see you."

"Okay." Callie looks around the group. "Where's Mommy?"

More sobs erupt from my colleagues, and I want to yell at them to stop. Callie doesn't need to hear that right now. Especially since I don't know what's going on. I can't assume the worst. I just can't.

"Come on over here," Pam says, holding her hand out for Callie. "We'll wait by the curb for Val to get here."

"Okay," Callie mumbles. Looking back at me, she smiles. "See you tomorrow, Miss Palmer."

"Right. See you tomorrow, little bean."

The minute, no, the second she's around the corner and out of sight, I lose it. I can't stop the torrent of tears. Nick wraps me up in his arms.

"She's dead."

It's not a question.

"Yes, baby."

"Who did it?"

"Her ex."

"Her ex? She's divorced?"

"In progress."

"He k-killed her?"

"He did."

I quickly pull away from him. "There were a lot of shots. Who else?"

"No other fatalities. Two wounded."

"Is *he* dead?" I hope so. I've never wanted anyone dead before, but I do now. "You got him?"

"Yes. I got him. Touch and go. He was still alive when they loaded him into the ambulance."

I've never felt prouder of someone in my life. Nick Martelli: Hero. "I hope he dies," I mutter. "Fucking asshole. Who else did he shoot?"

"I don't have names. No kids, though. His target was Mrs. Smart."

I place my hand over my heart, "Thank God, Nick. No kids." Thank God.

Nick pulls me into his chest, rubbing my back in a soothing way. "Thank God." His voice is soft, like a breath.

"Martelli!" shouts a man from somewhere behind me. "Time to move out."

Patting my back, Nick pulls away. "I've got to go to the station. I've got reports to file."

"No," I whine.

"I'll call you the minute I'm done. I'll come get you."

I nod, feeling a little lost. A *lot* lost. "I need to check on my kids. Make sure they're all picked up."

"I'll call you."

"And I'll wait for you to call."

Squeezing my shoulder, Nick moves toward his group of fellow first responders.

"My hero," I say quietly.

"Everyone's hero, Keels." Michael wraps his arm around me. "If you don't marry him, I will."

I snicker and immediately feel guilty. I can't laugh right now. But I want to thank Michael for making me feel something other than fear and sadness. "Let's go check on the kids."

"All gone. Every one of their parents was here."

"Even Augustus's?" His folks aren't the most diligent when it comes to their kid.

"Even Augustus's."

"Now what?" I turn to the other faculty.

Michael responds, "Pam wants to meet with us as soon as

Callie's picked up. We can't get back into the building, so we're meeting out back, out of sight of the news." He looks up just as the channel five helicopter zooms overhead.

Oh, I hadn't even noticed them. Of course they're here.

I grasp Michael's hand, and we walk slowly back to the playground, awaiting Principal Pam.

CHAPTER TWENTY-THREE

Nick

SEVERAL HOURS and after about a million forms have been completed, Captain Morgan has us all gather in the squad room. "You saved lives, Martelli."

When the clapping starts, I think I blush a little bit. I'm sure I did some good. Maybe saved lives, just not *everyone's* life. "Thanks." I nod. "Thanks." I hate this kind of shit. I was just doing my job. Literally. Also, I happened to be in the right place at the right time.

"Unfortunately, you're on paid administrative leave until the investigation is over. Standard procedure. Log in your weapon."

I'm aware of all that. "Right."

"Get your shit and get out of here. I'll call when you can come back. A week, tops."

"Right."

Grabbing a few things from my desk, I wave as I exit the

main room of Page P.D. Several guys, Joel for one, pat me on the back. "Nice job, man. Murphy's later?"

"Not tonight." I've got to take care of my girl. She was pretty freaked out today. "I'll give you a call."

"Right on, man."

I jog out the door to my SUV. Once the door's shut, I grab my phone.

Me: Where are you?

Keely: Home. Finally! I've just spent the last hour being inter-rogated by the Palmer clan.

Me: On my way. Pack a bag.

I half expect her to argue, so I'm surprised when she replies:

Keely: Okay.

She's waiting for me near the parking lot, suitcase in hand. Pulling up to her, I jump out of the car, rounding to her side. Opening the door, I grasp her suitcase. "Hop in. I've got your bag."

Keely nods. She's not smiling.

I place her suitcase in the back and shut the door. Once inside, I look over at her. "You okay?"

"No."

Nodding, I start my vehicle up. "You hungry?"

"No." She shakes her head. "I had a slice of pizza at my dad's."

"Does your sister, the roommate, know you're staying with me?"

"I just told her I would be with a friend."

A friend? Hmm. "Good." What else can I say? I know she's

not mentally in a place to talk about this, so I'll just drive us to my place. I'll make us some food. She needs to eat. Luckily, I bought groceries this weekend, so I'm all stocked up. If she doesn't like my options, we can order in.

Pulling into my driveway, I can't help feeling like Keely is a ticking time bomb. Sure, she cried at school and she may have cried around her family, but today's events were traumatic. Not just for her, but for her charges, her students. That adds to the stress she's probably feeling.

She opens her door and slides out before I can say anything. I jump out and retrieve her suitcase. Unlocking my front door, I wait for her to step in first. "I'll take your suitcase into the bedroom. Be right back."

Keely nods. Still silent.

Tick tock.

I speed walk into my bedroom. I reach for my pistol to place it into my gun safe but remember it was confiscated. That's procedure after a shooting. Kicking off my shoes, I quickly unbuckle my belt and holster and place it on top of my dresser. Pulling off my shirt and pants, I replace them with a T-shirt and sweats.

I race back to the living room, half expecting her to be sitting in a chair or on the couch, but she's hasn't budged from the spot by the door.

Tick tock.

Without another word, I approach her slowly. I place one arm behind her back and the other beneath her knees. When I lift her, I hear her release a jagged breath.

Tick tock.

I choose my large recliner. Walking there, I turn and sit. It's a chair for a big man, so it easily fits me with Keely on my lap. Pulling her closer, I say, "Put your arms around my neck, sweetie."

She does it silently.

Once I've got her comfortable on my lap, I begin to rock while running my palms over her legs and back. I feel her relax into me. Her nose is nuzzled up against my neck.

"I was so scared, Nick." Her voice is a mere whisper.

"I know." I rub her back slowly, up to her hairline, then back down to her waist. And then I repeat, "I know."

"I feel bad for Becca but so relieved my friends and kids are all okay. I feel selfish."

"Not selfish. Human."

"You saved my life. Our lives, Nick."

"*You* saved your life, babe. You saved your kids. *You* did that."

"What would I have done if you hadn't been there to tell me what to do?"

"Between you and Michael, you would have figured it out."

"I didn't even know those popping sounds were gunshots. Michael did, I guess."

"I'm positive you would've reacted the right way. The way you got the kids out the door, it was genius."

Lifting her head, she looks me in the eye. "What do you mean?"

I'm not surprised she doesn't remember. "You told them you were going back outside for a picnic and that the last one out was a rotten egg."

"I did?" She blinks a few times. "I don't remember saying that."

"Well, you did. You got them to safety, Keely."

A tear slides out of her eye. "I was so scared."

I place my palm on her head to urge it back down onto my shoulder. "Go ahead and let it out, Keely. Say or do what you need to do. I'm here. I'm not going anywhere." Ever.

I rock her as she cries and talks. She tells me what they did as soon as they were outside, how Mrs. Silver deserves a medal and that she'll love her forever, and how Michael kept her focused. "He told me if I didn't marry you, he would." She chuckles and I stop moving for a second.

"Oh. I—" Keely stammers. "I mean—"

"No. I like the sound of that."

"You want to marry Michael?" She titters again, and it sounds nice.

"No. Not what I meant." I start to rock again, using my hands to comfort her.

"I need a shower," she says in my ear.

I need one too, but I'm not about to take advantage of her in this state of mind. I'll hold her for as long as she needs but that's all. For now.

"You go shower. I'll make us something to eat. I'm starving. How 'bout you?"

"No. Not really."

"I'll whip up some pasta. If you feel like eating, there'll be plenty for both of us. How's that?"

"Okay." Keely slides from my lap.

"Towels, washcloths, everything you need are under the sink in the bathroom."

"Thanks, Nick."

"My pleasure, Keely."

I watch her walk down the hallway to my bedroom. As soon as the door shuts, I move to the kitchen. In no time I've got sauce bubbling and noodles boiling in another pot on the stove. I'm about to slice up some bread for toasting when I realize it's been a good thirty minutes since she went in to shower. Turning down the flame on my pots, I walk down the hall to my bedroom. Pushing my door open, I peek inside. Keely is on my bed, sleeping. Stepping closer, I can see her hair is wet. She showered and changed into sleep shorts and a tank top.

Grasping the throw from the end of my bed, I bring it up and cover her with it. She needs sleep. If she gets a little now, it'll help her in the long run. I doubt she'll sleep long, though.

In the kitchen, I rule out the bread and fill a plate with noodles and sauce. I turn everything off and cover each pot with a lid.

I place my plate on the counter and eat in silence. Alone, just like I normally do. Once I'm done, I rinse my dish and slide it into the dishwasher. I make my way into the bedroom and note the time. It's not quite seven. The sun hasn't even gone down yet. No matter. I slide in behind Keely, place my hand on her hip, and fall fast asleep.

CHAPTER TWENTY-FOUR

KEELY

I WAKE UP IN A STRANGE, dark room thanks to a bad dream. I blink a few times while attempting to remember. When I do, I have to catch my breath. *The shooting.* I feel a warm hand move down my hip to the side of my thigh and back up.

"Bad dream?"

Nick. I'm in bed next to Nick Martelli. I'd like to tell you my first instinct is to get up and run home, but that's not what I'm feeling. Instead of bolting like I'd normally do, I scoot closer to him. "Yeah."

His big, warm hand slides around my stomach to my belly button. He nudges me back, letting me know I can get closer. So I do, except I roll over to face him. He moves to his back, so I rest my head on that spot between his shoulder and chest. My head fits perfectly there. I bring my hand up to rest on his shirt-clad stomach. I want to feel his skin, so I move down to the bottom of his tee and slide my hand beneath it. Once I feel him, the rough hairs on his chest, I sigh. Moving my palm up and down his chest. I find myself falling back asleep.

CHAPTER TWENTY-FIVE

Nick

IT'S BEEN twenty-four hours since Keely walked into my place. I told her first thing this morning that I was on administrative leave. She told me school was canceled until further notice. That is, until the school was cleaned and the damage from the gunshots was repaired, and after Becca's funeral.

I expected Keely to ask me to take her home this morning, but she didn't. Instead, she sat at my small breakfast bar and watched me make us pancakes for breakfast. After that, I told her I was going to take a quick shower. When I stepped out of my en suite into my bedroom, Keely was sitting on my bed facing the bathroom. In the afternoon, I decided to relax on the sofa. She sat next to me and then burrowed against my chest. She slept there like that for over an hour.

Keely helped me make lunch. Nothing fancy, grilled cheese and tomato soup. We ate next to each other at my small dining table. I decided to get some work done in my office. Keely went with me, choosing to sit in the chair opposite and read one of my mom's old books. Jane Austen, I think.

When I asked if she felt like steak for dinner, she sat on my back patio watching me cook. In essence, she stayed either next to me or only a foot or two away from me all day.

The next day, it was more of the same. She never left my sight. When I suggested she take a nice hot bath, she asked me, rather shyly, if I'd sit in the bathroom and talk to her. Of course, I did as she asked. I sat on my vanity counter as she lathered up and relaxed in the warm bubbles. We talked about movies and music. Nothing serious. That afternoon, I pulled out some old board games I had in the closet. We played Sorry first. She kicked my ass. Then I got my deck of cards out and poker chips and schooled her on Five-card Stud. We joked and laughed all afternoon. It felt good. But her need to be close to me wasn't lost on me. I knew why she was doing it; I made her feel safe.

Ordinarily, I would have gotten off on that, but not like this. I'd had enough training on PTSD to know that keeping her cooped up in my house wasn't the answer. So, after the cards were put away, I asked her if she'd like to invite someone over. Like her sisters or her friends from school.

"Not my sisters." She looked at me and grimaced. "I haven't talked about you yet."

I can't tell you how much that bothers me, but I told her I'd give her time.

"How 'bout Michael?"

"Maybe. Can I think about it?"

"Sure. If you invite them, I can cook some of my mom's famous lasagna for everyone."

"I love lasagna."

I know.

"Let me send them a text."

"While you do that, I'll make us some lunch. Turkey sandwich okay?"

"Sure. Thank you."

I walk into my kitchen and round the breakfast bar and see she's already seated at the counter. At least she's got her phone out, typing away.

Her phone chimes, and she looks down at it. She doesn't smile, merely nods. "Michael can come."

What about your other friends?"

"I'm waiting to hear from them."

"Mayo?" I've yet to hear how she prefers some of these food basics.

Her little nose scrunches up. "No! Yuk."

No mayo. Noted.

I slide a plate over to her with a plain turkey and swiss on wheat. "Condiments are here." I point to mustard, butter, pickles, lettuce, tomato, and that dastardly mayonnaise.

"Thanks, Nick." I watch her top her turkey and cheese with lettuce, tomato, and yellow mustard.

I'm learning new things about her every day.

Keely takes a big bite of her sandwich, giving me a moan of approval. At least she's still got an appetite. That's good.

Her phone chimes several times.

"Sally can't come. But Julia and Kimberly are free."

"Great. Tell them six thirty."

"Here." She hands me her phone. "Type in your address for them, would ya?"

I type in the address and the time. Julia quickly responds asking what she can bring.

Nothing, I state. *We've got it.*

We've. I like the sound of Keely and me as a we.

At least we *will.* Keely and I need to take a run to the store. Getting her out of the house will be a positive step for her.

I CAN HEAR the three of them laughing from the kitchen. I've spent the better part of the afternoon preparing the lasagna. A masterpiece takes time, after all. When her friends arrived, I served them wine and told them to make themselves comfortable. The minute they were all back together, I left them alone. They had things to talk about related to the shooting and I knew if they had questions for me, they'd ask.

As I predicted, I overheard them talking about the events, so I moved to my right to keep an eye on Keely. She began to ask questions, since she and Michael were both out of the building when it started.

"Kim, your room was close to Becca's. Did you see anything?"

She nods. "I heard shouting in the hallway. I stepped up to my door and peeked out the small window in the door. I could see the back of Becca and part of Phil, her husband."

It's Julia's turn to ask a question. "Did you see the gun?"

"No. I saw both of his hands, though. He was flapping them around angrily. He was screaming at Becca. Cussing loud enough for my kids to hear, so I asked all of them to move to the back of the room to the reading center, thinking that would help, but we could still hear him."

"What was he saying?" asks Michael.

"Just ranting about her leaving him but mostly about Callie and her taking Callie away from him." She pauses, then adds, "When I heard the first popping sound, I wasn't sure what it was, but one of my kids recognized it as a gunshot."

"What did you do?" asks Michael.

"I'm lucky; I've got an emergency exit in my room, so I immediately had the kids move out the back door. I told them to get low and move along the side of the building. As soon as we were far enough away, we ran for the baseball field and hid behind the dugout until we heard the sirens."

One of them adds, "That was smart, Kimberly." I'm not sure which one.

"What about you, Julia?" asks Keely.

"Since my room was all the way on the opposite end of the building, the popping sounds were barely loud enough for me to hear. The kids could hear it though. We got up and went out the door near my room and made it to the bus garage and hid there."

"How did her husband even get in the building?" asks Keely.

Kim answers, "He just signed in. Nobody knew about the separation."

"I heard there was a restraining order," Julia interjects.

Keely says, sounding shocked, "What? Did Pam know?"

Julia again. "Apparently not. He signed in saying he was having lunch with Callie."

"Shit. So careless," mutters Keely.

"Sad is what it is," Michael says softly.

Julia asks the group, "How are Cliff and Maureen?"

Cliff Johnson and Maureen Gibbons were both wounded at the scene.

Michael responds, "I talked to Maureen's husband, and he said she was in a lot of pain but doing okay after the surgery."

"What about Cliff?"

I can't tell who asked that.

"I heard he lost half his foot." Kimberly is the one talking now.

"Oh, no," Keely says. "He's our P.E. teacher. He needs his foot."

"I heard they were shot trying to subdue him. Is that true?" I think it's Julia asking, but she sounds an awful lot like Kim.

Michael answers this one. The guy knows it all. "That's

true. They tried to get the gun away from him. They were shot during the struggle. Cliff was shot in the foot, and Maureen was hit in the hip."

There's mumbling until one of them announces, "Becca's funeral. It's slated for this Saturday."

Just then, I step into the room to place a tray of antipasto along with small plates, napkins, and utensils on the coffee table. Michael turns to me, asking, "What have you heard about Becca's husband?"

There's only so much I can tell them. "He was rushed into surgery to remove two bullets. The other was a through-and-through."

"And?" Keely asked. "Did he *die*?" The way she said "die" nearly made me shiver. It was filled with vitriol.

"He made it through surgery. The last I heard, he was in critical condition." I was also informed that one of my bullets nicked his spinal column, and at this point, he still had no feeling in his lower extremities, but the asshole will live. Unfortunately for him, it'll be in a federal prison.

"Good," hisses my girl.

"Keely." The woman who I think is Kimberly reaches out, touching her arm.

"No. He killed Becca. He could have killed our kids. He doesn't deserve to live." Keely stands suddenly and looks down at her friend. "Are you defending him?"

"No." Her friend leans forward. "Of course not. I just know it does no good to... to hate. It won't bring her back, and it'll only make you unhappy."

"Serious?" Keely's getting upset. "Your room was right next to the art room, Kim. You could have been k-killed." I hear her voice break.

I move to her, but Kim beats me to it. Wrapping her friend up in her arms, she holds Keely tight, "I know, honey. I know. I was scared. If it wasn't for Officer Hottie over there, we'd have been screwed."

"True." Michael holds up his wineglass. "To Officer Hot Stuff."

I wish I could avoid this. "I just did my job."

"Not just that," adds Julia. "Because of the safety training, I knew what to do in my classroom. We got the fuck out of there. I don't think I would have done that if you hadn't told us to save ourselves first."

Keely pulls away from Kimberly, steps over to me, and wraps her arms around me. "He's a hero." She says it quietly but loud enough for her friends to hear.

"I was just doing my job."

"You should do that training at every school, Nick."

I look at the three of them, not knowing who suggested it.

"I should." I really should.

"You should, baby." Keely says sweetly.

She called me baby, and it makes my dick hard. I can't wait to hear that again when we're alone.

Clearing my throat, I announce, "Dinner will be ready in fifteen minutes."

I kiss Keely's forehead and move back into the kitchen just as Michael whispers loud enough for me to hear, "Marry him or I will."

The hell he will. I chuckle as I work my magic in my kitchen.

CHAPTER TWENTY-SIX

KEELY

"I'M STUFFED." My God, my man can cook. I know my friends feel the same. Julia and Kimberly are both rubbing their stomachs like they're about to burst.

Shit. My man?

I look over at him as he laughs at something Michael just said. He's fit in seamlessly with my besties. Not that I didn't think he would, but seeing him here, with them... well, it's surreal.

Could I picture him with my sisters? My dad?

I blink and watch him tell some funny story about a rabid dog he encountered when he was a rookie beat cop in Phoenix.

The answer is yes. I could totally picture Nick with my family. My sisters would adore him. Not just because he saved my life and the lives of so many others, but because he's amazing. Smart, funny, handsome, protective Nick Martelli is the complete package. Not only that, I like him. Not only *that*, he makes me feel safe. So safe. It scares me to think of leaving his house without him. What happens when we have to go back to work? How will I do it? I know he can't come to school with me... but what if he could? Perhaps I could request constant "community outreach."

I shake my head, which draws Nick's attention. "You okay over there, babe?"

"Yeah." I look at him. I decide to just say it. "I'm scared to go back to school."

Before Nick can respond, my friends jump in.

"Me too," says Michael.

"I'm terrified," Julia says, and Kimberly nods.

"We'll all go together. I'm sure Sally feels the same, hon," Michael says, patting the top of my hand.

I nod and smile, but I'm not feeling at all sure about it. I'd still like Nick there too.

"I'll go in with you too," Nick says, looking at us one at a time.

"Good. It's a plan," Michael says, squeezing my hand now.

"Will you go to Becca's funeral with me too?" God, I'm fucking pathetic.

"Of course." Nick looks at me with such care. His eyes are soft and so understanding. I want to wrap myself up in him and never leave. Ever.

SAFE. I say it to myself as I'm cuddled up against a sleeping Nick Martelli. He's snoring just a little bit, which on any other boyfriend would be annoying as fuck. But on him? It's adorable. And yes, I said boyfriend, but that's not what I meant. Not really. It's just... I feel safe. I'm sorry I keep saying that but, right now, I'm scared shitless about going outside by myself. I'm terrified to go to school. Shit, if I'm that scared, think about my poor students.

No. I can't think about them right now. I'll cry.

Callie.

I feel my nose start to burn and my eyes water. That poor child. I may never see her again. Michael mentioned that Becca's sister Val has temporary custody of her, and that Val lives in another school district. Not far from Page, but far enough that I won't have her anymore. And honestly, I wouldn't want her to come back. Not to the place her mother was murdered by her fucking evil father.

And just like that, my tears are replaced with anger. I need to let it go. Kim was right; it does no one any good. I need to focus on my kiddos right now. I lift my head and look down at the sleeping god next to me. He's shirtless. The sheet is barely covering his lower half. I lift it up, and I'm a tad disappointed that he's wearing his boxers. Sliding my palm along his happy trail up over his navel to the middle of his chest, I run my fingers through the smattering of chest hair there. I move my hand to skim over his nipple. I feel him jolt slightly.

"Keely," he says in a husky, sleepy voice.

He sounds so damn sexy.

"Yeah?"

"What're you doing, honey?"

"Nothing." But that's not exactly the truth.

"Nothing?"

"Well, nothing but touching you."

As my hand moves over to his other nipple, Nick moves his big paw over mine, stopping its progress. "Baby. You've been through a lot."

I have, but why should that stop me from getting something I want? Maybe even need. "So?"

"So. You've had a trauma. I wouldn't feel right."

Ignoring him, I slide my body over until I'm nearly on top of him. I swing my leg over his hips and push myself up until I'm astride him. "Nick," I say, pulling off my tank top, "I need you."

It's no lie either. My body is wired, and there's nothing like an orgasm to calm me.

"Jesus, Keely." Nick sounds like he's against this, but the big rod thickening between my legs tells me another story. So do his hands the second he slides them from my rib cage up to cup my breasts.

"Nick." I let my head fall back. My hair is down, so I feel it tickle my lower back. "Pinch them." My boobs are super sensitive on a good day, and right now, they're doubly so.

"Call me baby," Nick says huskily as he pinches and tugs on my hard nipples.

"Baby," I whine. "Fuck me, baby. Please?"

In two seconds, I swear, Nick has me up to my knees and his boxers pushed down. "Turn around."

I know where he's going. He remembered my favorite position. Reverse cowgirl. I quickly rotate until my ass is facing him. "Scoot back."

Oh, shit. Is he?

I hear a tear and realize it was my underwear. A casualty of war, I guess. Not war. Love. Oh, shit. Not love. Lust. A casualty of lust. I reach down and pull away what is left of my second-favorite pair of panties just as Nick's hands reach around to my stomach and pull me back. "Let me taste you."

Hellz yeah. I scoot back, using his thighs as my support. The minute I'm over his mouth, I feel his tongue lick me. It's firm and it goes deep.

"Baby," I moan. "Yes."

He stops momentarily to grunt, "Suck my cock, Keely."

I look down at his engorged dick. It's practically vibrating, it's so hard. Fluid is already seeping out of the head. In the past,

I'd describe a man's penis as ugly, but not this one. No, Nick Martelli's dick is almost as perfect as the rest of him. Leaning down, I slide him into my mouth, sucking as I move down.

"Fuck. Jesus, Keely. Harder. Suck me harder."

Okay, truth? There's nothing hotter than a man like Nick being this needy. Plus, I sort of like his bossy side in bed. Only in bed though.

Reaching out, I grasp the base of his dick and squeeze. Sucking harder, I move down his shaft as far as I can go. I can't deep throat. My gag reflex just can't handle it, especially with a guy the size of Nick, so I use my hand too.

He must approve, because instead of working on me, he's muttering sweet nothings. You know, sweet nothings like, "You're the hottest fucking woman. Your mouth. Jesus, that mouth. Suck."

I stop because, well, because he did. I push myself up until I can look back at him.

"W-why'd you stop?" He's panting.

"Because you did. You started on such a good note, but now you just stopped."

Nick is looking at me and, at first, I'd say he was pissed. His dark brows are all scrunched up in the middle, nostrils flaring a little bit; but then they soften. It's like he remembered how this all started.

Gently, Nick slides his palms around my hips, then up until they're cupping my breasts, pinching my nipples. I moan.

"You're right, honey. I'm sorry. This is about you."

"No, it's not. It's about both of us."

"Scoot back up here. Let me get another taste of that delectable pussy."

I groan, because as crass as that sounded, I fucking loved it. I push my ass back up and move myself over him again. When I feel his mouth on me, I start to shiver. The little hairs all over my body come alive. His mouth moves over me. He nibbles on my outer lips and then his tongue slides into me, making me moan. One of his hands reaches down and slides through my crease until he locates my clit. Using his mouth and his hand, he pushes me into the abyss. The French call an orgasm *le petite mort,* or *little death.* I know why. That feeling when you tumble over that edge is like you're dying the most beautiful death. I swear my heart stopped beating for a split second. It feels so good; I want it again.

"More," I say, sounding like a very selfish wench.

Nick begins to lick between my folds, using his hands on my waist to hold me where he wants me. I peek down at his dick and decide it's his turn. I slide my tongue over the head of his cock, licking up the wetness there. Cupping his sac, I slide my mouth over the head and suck him just a little at first. I want to hear him beg me again. I guess I'll have to wait, because instead of begging he says, "Ride me, honey."

Pushing myself up to my knees, I scoot forward until I'm right above him. Nick's hand is holding his dick. Finding the right spot, I slowly begin to lower myself down onto him.

"Oh, Nick," I say in a high-pitched voice. A voice I don't recognize. But, damn, the man feels perfect.

I quickly press myself all the way down and then up again even faster. Leaning down, I place my hands on his thighs, using them for support. His hands are somewhere on my lower body, helping. In no time, Nick begins to thrust up as I push down. We're moving so damn fast. Nick's movements are hard. I push up so I can lean back a little—chasing down that *one* elusive spot. When I find it, I scream, "Yes!" as my clit makes contact with him over and over and over again. I come so hard I don't remember where the hell I am. I see stars, lights flashing. I've stopped moving, but Nick hasn't, pushing himself into me, harder and harder. He comes with a grunt. "Keely," he breathes. "Fuck."

"I know."

I'm panting as Nick twitches inside of me. I don't want to move, because even soft, he feels so damn good. But I'm probably crushing the poor guy. I move forward and lift myself up until I hear a wet popping sound as he pulls out. Then wetness falls out of me onto him and my legs.

I look down between us first, then peer over my shoulder at him. "No condom."

CHAPTER TWENTY-SEVEN

Nick

"NO CONDOM."

Keely's words are repeating around in my head. *"No condom."* I know we started to talk about going bare. "You said you were on birth control, yeah?"

"Yes." She sounds irritated, but then she sighs. "I started this. I should have brought it up. I was just too into it."

"I get it. Me too. But are you okay? With that?" I point down to where we were joined.

"Yes." She pauses. "No." Then she pauses again. "Yes."

Jesus. This woman. "Which is it, Keely?" I'm not angry, and I'm trying my best not to sound that way. I just need to know.

"Yes. I'm okay with it." She moves until she's essentially kneeling next to me. Looking into my eyes, she adds, "I want kids someday but not yet. I'm not ready."

"I feel the same way."

"Okay. Good. So, we're on the same page?"

"Same page." Well, I'd like kids right now, but this thing with Keely and me isn't official. Hell, she hasn't even told her family about me yet.

"Good." Keely nods and slides off the bed. "Let me get a washcloth."

Good idea. I'm sort of a mess. "Thanks, Keely."

"Welcome," she shouts from the bathroom.

Back in minutes, Keely proceeds to wash me with a warm washcloth. She's gentle, and it makes my eyes flutter shut. "You've got a pretty dick, Nick." Then she snorts, and it wakes me back up. "That rhymed."

"It sure did."

She laughs again. "I'm all sorts of awesome, Nick. Don't forget that."

"Never." I'd never forget all the sorts of awesome that is Keely May Palmer.

THE NEXT MORNING OVER COFFEE, I decide to ask Keely about the man who assaulted her sister. "You know?" I say but hesitate.

"Yeah?" Keely's doing something on her phone, not yet looking up at me.

"I've got time to do a search on Violet's attacker...."

"Yeah?" Keely places her phone on the table.

"Yeah, I do."

Blinking, Keely looks at my face then into my eyes. "Confidential? Between you and me?"

"Absolutely. I can call a buddy of mine down in Phoenix so no one here will even know about it."

Keely stares at my face some more. "Look. I still don't want you getting the cavalry involved. I haven't talked to Violet about you delving into this."

I watch her closely. I can practically see the wheels turning in her pretty head.

"Until then, you can just do a basic search."

"You mean like on Google?"

"Yeah. Google him." She pauses, waiting for my acquiescence.

I nod.

Stepping closer, she finally says, "His last name is Maines." She hesitates but then adds, "Kyle Maines."

"Be right back. I'll be in my home office."

"Can I come with you?"

She's either still feeling the need to be with me all the time, or she wants to hear this. "Sure."

I step into my office. Pulling another chair over next to mine, Keely sits at my desk as I google the name. When several photos emerge, I turn the computer so she can see the images. "Do you recognize him in any of these?"

"Well, I never actually saw him or a picture because Violet—it was too hard for her to see him, even a picture." She stands, then leans over the desk to peer at my computer. I watch as Keely gasps and her eyes grow round in horror. "Shit. Shit, shit, shit."

"What?"

Pointing to a dark-headed male, Keely wheezes, "That guy. I've seen him before."

"Where?"

"Here!" she shouts. "In Page!" Moving away from my desk, she starts to pace in front of it. Back and forth like a caged animal. "At Murphy's, I think." Stopping suddenly, she turns to face me. She looks terrified, horrified. "He-he walked up to our table. He talked to Vi." Keely literally screams. "He had the fucking nerve to c-c-come up to our table. To talk to her."

"When was this?"

"Shit. Shit, fucking, motherfucker. I'm going to fucking kill him, Nick." I've never seen her this angry. I jump up and race round the desk, pulling her into my arms. Yanking away from me, she starts to pace again. "He fucking walked right up to her and said something smarmy." Her lip flares in disgust. "We all thought he was good-looking."

"When was this?"

"Like a month ago. A little more. We all noticed Violet's reaction. Hell, we've talked about it since then. Not with her, but Lainie and I have wondered if it was someone she'd consider dating. We all want her to be happy—to find her person."

I'm trying to figure out what to do when I watch Keely collapse to the ground.

She's in a ball on the ground, and I hear her sob. "I fucking tried to en-encourage her that night. Teasing her about a guy hitting on her."

"You didn't know."

"I knew what she'd been through. She looks up at me. "But she said his name, 'Kyle.' I should have known. Her face got so fucking red, Nick. She ran off to the bathroom. I thought she was just freaked out about a guy noticing her since..."

Pounding the floor with her fist, she starts to cry again. "He followed her."

"Home?"

"No. Back to the bathroom." Keely sobs again. "Why didn't I notice?"

I move down to the floor with her. "You were at Murphy's. Having a good time. You didn't know. She didn't tell you. Give yourself a break, baby. You've been through so much this week. Give yourself a break."

Before I know it, Keely has crawled into my lap. Her face is in my neck, arms and legs wrapped around me. "I'm the worst sister in the entire world."

"Shh." I rub both hands up and down her back. "Violet understands. I'm sure she didn't want you to worry."

That makes her cry harder. I decide to shut up and just comfort her.

CHAPTER TWENTY-EIGHT

KEELY

Me: Vi. I... we need to talk.

I WAIT FOR SEVERAL MINUTES, but she doesn't respond.

Me: Text me when you have time. Love you.

Still no response. I know she's not mad at me. Hell, she doesn't even know I know. But, the fact remains, I'm the worst sister in the entire world. And no, I can't give that moniker to any of my other siblings, because I'm literally the only one who knows or knew about Kyle. But, being the self-absorbed bitch that I am, I couldn't tell the difference between an embarrassed Violet and a terrified one. She can't trust me to know when she's scared out of her wits. No wonder she didn't confide in me, then or now. Hell, I don't even know everything that went down that night; she was so tight-lipped. I told her talking about it would help. But I guess I can't blame her. Reliving something like that, even to her twin, would be horrible.

God, I want to kill that asshole. I don't even care how. I could run him over with my car, but I'm not sure that'd be satisfying enough. Maybe stab him with a letter opener. Or better yet, an ice pick. That'd be nice. I sure as hell know he's too good for a gun. Too fast. No, this motherfucker deserves to suffer. Now I just need to find him.

Wait! What if he lives in Page or nearby? What if the whole reason he was here was because of Violet? No. He wouldn't. It had to be a coincidence. But I need to be sure.

Sliding off Nick's bed, I go in search of him. After my meltdown in his office, Nick tucked me into bed and told me to sleep. That he'd call his friend in Phoenix and see what he can find out about Kyle. When I looked at the clock, I notice that I actually slept for over an hour. I feel better, sort of. Not great, but better.

My first stop—Nick's home office. He's not there. Next, I check the kitchen, walk past the hall bathroom, then I hear clinking coming from his garage. Opening the side door, I peer out to see Nick lying back on a weight machine. He's pumping a long barbell with several large weights on either end. Not wanting to startle him, I walk over until we're facing one another. I stare as his muscles bulge and the sweat pours down his forehead. He's wearing a tank and some athletic shorts. My God, this man... so gorgeous. But, no.

This isn't about me.

Without prelude, I ask, "What did you find out?" I asked him if he could find out where Kyle lived. I wanted to be sure he wasn't in Page.

Grunting, Nick places the barbell onto its holder and pushes himself up to sitting. His ab muscles flex beneath his sweaty tank. Nick uses the bottom of his shirt to wipe his face. "Let's go inside. I need a drink."

Uh-oh. I can tell by his tone of voice this isn't going to be good, and the fact that we have to sit down is a double whammy.

With a bottle of water in one hand and my other fisting the bottom of my shorts, I watch as Nick gulps down most of his drink.

"Well?" Jesus, he's taking his sweet ass time.

"Kyle Maines. Twenty-seven. Son of William Maines and Frances Abernathy."

I blink at his words. "Abernathy." The name sounds familiar.

"Lieutenant Governor Frances Abernathy."

"Lieutenant Governor?"

"Prior to that, she was a state senator." He pauses. "And at the time of your sister's assault, she was the Pima County District Attorney."

"Pima County?"

"Tucson."

"Uh-huh." I stand up quickly. "Now it all makes sense. I know how this works. His mommy is a bigwig with the state of Arizona, so he gets to do whatever the fuck he wants. Like rape sweet, unassuming girls like my sister."

"Keely."

"What!" I snap, rearing back at him. "It isn't fair."

"I know. But can you just—"

"What? Let it go? Forget about it?"

"No. Listen to me, please."

I shake my head, but I stay quiet. I want to hear what he has to say.

"He lives in Sedona."

"Fuck." Like an hour from here.

"He works for an insurance company there. In sales."

"Sales." I don't know why that's relevant.

"Traveling sales. It's probably why he was in Page. For work."

I guess that's a relief. He wasn't here for my sister. "Does he come here a lot?"

"I've got a call in to another friend of mine about that. He can check it out without drawing attention to us."

"Alright. What else?"

Nick holds his hand out to me, so I take it. Pulling me into him, he places his hands on my hips. "Guys like him, like Kyle..."

"Yeah?"

"They..." Nick pauses.

"What?"

"There are usually others."

"Other girls?"

"Yes. Think about it. He's an asshole. His mom's prominent and powerful."

"Which means he gets away with murder."

"It's just a hunch, but if there are other accusations, I won't be able to leave it alone. He's dangerous."

"What are you saying?" I'm afraid to ask but I need to know.

"Violet may need to know what's happening in case he..."

"Retaliates?"

"Maybe. But if we arrest and charge him, she may have to testify."

Oh, motherfucking fucker. "She won't."

"She may have to. She was willing to do it at the time."

"That was before the fucking cops made her feel like it was her fault!" I'm yelling at him. At Nick. I've pulled away from him, and I'm yelling at him at the top of my lungs. He looks hurt even though he's trying to school his expression. I can't help it though. Sisters before misters. My sisters mean the world to me.

All of them are. I'd never have made it this far without them. Not after Mom died.

I turn away from him and walk to his bedroom. He's following me. "Keely."

"No. I need to go. I need to talk to Violet." I grab my suitcase, unzip it, and throw whatever is nearby inside. I'll get the rest some other time. Maybe Nick can drop it off somewhere. At school maybe. Zipping up my bag and without looking at him, I ask, "Can you take me home, please?"

"Sure, baby. I'll take you home."

Oh, shit. He sounds so sad. Hot tears slide out of my eyes like they're escaping prison. He doesn't deserve this from me. He's been nothing but perfect, honorable, sweet, and brave for me. I don't deserve Nick Martelli.

"Nick?"

"Yep," he says curtly.

"Please don't do anything yet. Let me talk to Vi."

Nick nods, and a sense of relief hits me. I know it's short-lived relief, but I'll take it.

ONCE I'M HOME and alone in my bedroom, I press Violet's number. It rings three or four times and I'm wondering if I need to just head over to her place and see if she's home. When she finally answers, she sounds out of breath.

"Hey, hon. How are you?"

She's worried about *me*. Figures. "I'm fine. Good." I pause because I need to figure out how to start this off. "Um, I need to talk to you about that night at Murphy's."

"Which one?" she chuckles. "We go a lot."

"That's true." I attempt to laugh but it's not happening. "The one with Kyle."

I hear Violet's gasp and wish I was there in person. I should have gone over to her place. This isn't something I should have done over the phone. Her deep breath is audible. "I know the night."

"Why didn't you tell me?" Shit. This isn't about me. "I mean, why didn't you talk to me or one of us. If I'd known, I'd have..."

"You would have killed him."

She's right.

"And that would have been bad?" My laugh this time is bitter. "I would have kicked his fucking ass, for sure."

"Then, you'd be in jail right now."

"I. Don't. Care." I say a little too loudly. "I'd go to jail for you, Vi. That fucking rapist needs to pay." I'm doing my best to stay calm, but that's out the window now.

"I needed time to process it in my own way, Keely."

"So, you've had time to process it. What've you figured out?"

She remains silent.

"Nick knows." More silence. I can't tell if she's angry or what. I should have fucking done this in person. "He wants to investigate."

"He does? How..."

I wait for the rest of the question.

"Are you seeing Nick?"

"We're friends, I guess." Because I'm not ready to talk to Violet about Nick, I quickly add, "Kyle lives in Sedona."

"Oh."

"Yeah." I swallow deeply before I continue. "He thinks he's probably done it to others."

Violet sniffles on the other end. If I were there, I could be hugging her right now. "Do you want me to come over there?"

"No. I'm okay. It's just..."

"What?"

"I think Nick should investigate. I'm ready to move on with my life, and I can't if this is still out there. If *he's* still out there. I'm tired of being scared."

"Yeah?" Thank goodness.

"Yeah."

"I love you, Vi."

"I love you more, Keels. Thank you for asking Nick for help. I don't deserve you."

And there it is. That's Violet for you. She's making me feel better. "No. I don't deserve you."

CHAPTER TWENTY-NINE

KEELY

THE CASKET IS OPEN.

God, I hate funerals. I especially hate this one. Everyone, and I mean everyone, from Page is here. There's barely room to stand in this place. I wish I could be hidden in the back somewhere with my family, but Becca's sister wanted her teacher family near the front. I'm two rows behind Callie. I want to wrap her up in my arms and tell her it's all going to be okay. I know what it's like to lose a mom. But she lost both of her parents. She'll, hopefully, never have to look at her father's fucking face ever again. No kid should have to deal with that bullshit.

I catch her looking back at me, her little eyes red from crying. I give her a weak smile and hold up both of my hands, making them into the shape of a heart. "I love you," I mouth silently to her. She nods, then turns, facing forward.

As soon as the service is over, we file out to our cars. I'm riding with Michael, Julia, Sally, and Kimberly out to the burial site. I'd like to skip this part. Watching a casket getting lowered into the ground is beyond dreadful, and the fact that Callie has to watch her mother's body move slowly down into the earth is too much for me. I know. I remember like it was yesterday— throwing a flower on her casket. Then I watched as people tossed dirt on the top of it. God, I wanted to jump down on top of her pretty wooden box and go with her. To cling to those metal handles on the sides and stay there forever. I bet that's how Callie feels too. I know it.

I haven't stopped crying since I stepped foot into the church and saw Becca lying there in her favorite flowered dress. I know it's her favorite because she wore it mostly on Mondays. She said it cheered her up. Beside her are drawings done by some of her art students, all saying how much they love her. In her hand is a photo of Callie along with a folded piece of paper. I can't get a word out without blubbering. Becca looks pretty, but there's something so unnatural about looking at a person in a casket. Her coloring is wrong. She'd never have worn that shade of lipstick. She was an apple-red lipstick kind of woman. Sassy. Becca was sassy.

The minute the burial is over, I race back to Michael's car. Sliding inside, I lay my head back onto the headrest, concentrating on getting my shit together.

"The hard part is over," says Julia as she slides in next to me.

"I know."

"We need to go back to the church for the luncheon."

I groan. "I know."

I SEE him as soon as we walk in the door. He's in a suit and tie, and I swear to all that's holy my ovaries explode at the sight of him. He's wearing a dark gray jacket and pants paired with a light gray shirt and a tie swirled with all sorts of colors, but mostly grays. Nick Martelli looks like sex on legs, sinful. I walk toward him without another thought. He deserves to know I don't blame him. That I know it's his job to hunt down criminals like Kyle Maines. I let him do it, after all. I set it all in motion the second I gave him the name.

All it means is that we can't be together. Not anymore. Because the minute he brings Violet into this shitstorm, she'll need me full time. And I will not choose a man over my twin. Ever.

"Hi, Nick."

"Hey, beautiful." He leans in like he wants to kiss me, but I pull away. His head moves back quickly once he sees my reaction.

"You look nice," I say softly.

"Thanks. You do too."

Releasing a breath I didn't know I was holding, I say, "Look—"

"You must be our hero." I recognize the voice.

Nick holds out his hand. "Nick Martelli."

"Agatha Palmer." She hip-checks me. "I'm this one's older sister."

I smile, because Aggie has gotten so much more extroverted since she met her man, Ian. I love it.

"Nice to meet you, Agatha."

Ian steps up beside her, holding his hand out too. "Ian Burke. You must be Nick Martelli."

Nick looks a little confused, so I explain, "Ian is Agatha's boyfriend."

"Oh, right."

"Ex-FBI," Ian says proudly. "Retired."

Nick nods.

"You okay after everything?"

Nick nods. "I am. Thanks for asking. I'm more concerned about Keely."

"Oh?" Agatha perks up. "Why?" She adds, "I mean, I know why. It was traumatic, but is she okay?" She looks me over like she's searching out obvious injuries.

"No, it's just as you said; it was traumatic. For all of them."

"I heard the husband wanted to attend the funeral," Ian says softly.

"What!" I shout it so loudly that everyone turns to look in our direction. Hissing as quietly as possible, I lean in, "Are you fucking kidding me?"

"Not uncommon," Nick mumbles.

"He wanted to be here for Callie," Ian adds.

I place my hands over my face. I'm so pissed, I want to scream. Pulling them away, I glare at Nick, then at Ian. "He caused this."

"Babe," Nick begins, but I cut him off.

"I know. I get it." I'm angry. So angry. And he called me babe in front of my sister. "I gotta go."

I turn on my heel and march out the door into the hot Arizona sun. I only live about three miles from the church. A walk will do me good. I should call or text Michael, since he was my ride, but I don't want to. I don't want to see anyone. I need to be alone. I need to mentally prepare for two days from now, when I have to step foot back into that school.

I WAKE up to complete darkness. I look down at myself and see I'm still wearing my funeral dress. The only things I took off were my heels. I've got blisters now, thanks to the fact I thought it was a great idea to walk home. And three miles was a little shy of the actual distance. I'd say it was closer to five. It took me almost two hours to get here, even though I cut through lawns and a couple of parking lots to make it shorter.

My phone buzzed and rang nonstop after I left the church. It got so annoying, I just turned the fucking thing off. Now I feel bad about that. I'm sure they were just worried. They didn't deserve to be worried. Reaching out, I feel around the bed for my purse or phone. Either one would work, but it's not there. I slide off my bed, but the second I step on the ground, I nearly crumple. My feet. Fuck, I really messed up my feet.

I opt for crawling out to the living room. I do so slowly, since my toes are rubbing on the carpet, making them hurt even more. I've got no choice; I need to keep moving. When I'm down the hall and almost to my living room where I'm sure I left my purse, I see feet. Well, not feet, shoes. I see black leather shoes. Men's black leather shoes. They're attached to long legs clad in dark gray fabric.

Pushing back onto my heels, I blink at Nick's face.

"How did you get in here?"

"Your sister."

"Lainie?"

"Yes."

"She let you in here?"

"Yes."

"Why?"

Nick stands up quickly and takes the two steps toward me. Glaring down at me, he looks so damn pissed. "Because, fuck." He runs his hands through his hair, then his eyes are back down on me. "I was fucking crazy worried about you. No one could find you. You wouldn't answer your fucking phone, Keely." He stomps away from me, then back. "You're a self-centered brat."

"What?!" He didn't just say that. "I am not." I think of others. I really do.

"You are. You just survived a school shooting and you have the fucking nerve to walk away, scaring everyone who lo—cares about you."

"I just needed to get out of there!" I shout loudly. "I'm a grown-up. I don't need permission to be alone." I move up from my knees and wince. The pain nearly causes me to fall back to the ground, but I make myself stand. Moving to the chair across from the sofa, I sit down.

"What's wrong with your feet?" he asks, sounding less mad.

"Blisters. I'm fine. I can take care of myself." I'm not going to cry. I'm not going to cry.

"Jesus," Nick mutters. He moves in front of me, squatting down until we're at eye level. "I'm going to say some things. I need you to just listen. Then I'll leave. Okay?"

Why did hearing him say he's leaving make my heart hurt? "Okay."

"I'm not giving up on you, Keely. But I am going to give you the space you need. I tried to do that before, but I couldn't seem to stick to the plan. I will now. I want you. All of you. That includes your family. I don't want to be a dirty secret. I want it all, but until you decide to make that happen, there is no us."

"No us?"

"If you can't ever see yourself doing that—introducing me to your family as your man, tell me. It'll hurt less if you just tell me."

Hurt less? *I'm* hurting *him*?

"Nick," I whimper. He takes a deep breath, standing up to his full height. I have to look way up at his face.

"I'll meet you at the front entrance of the school on Monday morning."

"Oh."

"I promised you I'd walk you inside, and I won't let you down."

I know he won't. I nod.

"I mean it, Keely. I want it all." He starts to walk to the door, but he hesitates and turns back. "I've never told another woman that, Keely. I've never wanted anyone but you."

Oh. Shit. Tears start flowing, and I don't see them stopping. Ever.

CHAPTER THIRTY

Nick

IT FEELS good to be back to work. The captain called me on Sunday and told me I'd been reinstated starting first thing Monday morning. When I told him I'd be at the station late and the reason, he was a little emotional.

"Of course. That's a great idea, son. Community outreach at its finest. I'll have other units there as well."

"Yes, sir." I pause. "I was thinking I'd dress in street clothes for it."

"Why's that, son?"

"Well, I was thinking it could be scary for the kids—seeing all of us there in uniform again."

"Ah, I see. What if a few of us dressed in uniform and asked the others to wear street clothes? Then it won't look like it did that day."

"That's a good plan, sir. Thank you."

"I'm proud of you, Nick. I feel fortunate you chose to come to Page."

"Thank you, sir."

"And I'm sure you'll make that young lady an excellent husband." Captain Morgan chuckles.

"When she's ready, I hope so, sir."

I'm at the school early. I wasn't sure what time the teachers would arrive, so I erred on the side of caution. At seven sharp, I park my cruiser in front of the school to notify and reassure people there is a police presence here.

The first car pulls into the lot fifteen minutes later. It's Principal Pamela Moynihan. I step out of my vehicle to greet her, shaking her hand just as several additional police cruisers pull into the lot. One of them carries Captain Morgan. He shakes the principal's hand, asking her how she's holding up.

"Sir," I say in greeting. I look behind him to see Joel, Mark, Stan, and Amy. "Hey," I say as casually as possible.

"Pam, we'd like to escort your teachers and the kids into the building, if that's okay with you."

"Wonderful. Thank you. If they're half as nervous as I am...." She smiles. "I've been here all weekend and my nerves are still shot."

"Understandable," says Mark. "We've got your back."

I see the emotion all over Pam's face. "Be brave," she says quietly, and then adds, "Not you. You're already brave, Officer Martelli. I'm saying that for myself."

I nod and smile at her. I get it.

We don't have to wait long for cars to begin pulling into the lot. When I spot the light blue Honda, my heart thumps loudly in my chest. It was the right thing to do on Saturday. I had to do it. When she's ready, I'll be here.

En masse, the teachers of Page Elementary walk toward us.

Most of them are holding hands, and some have arms around each other. Stopping in front of Pam, the group waits.

Pam looks emotional, but she's holding it together. "You are the heart and soul of this school," she says to her teachers and staff. "Our children need you. Be strong, but don't hesitate to let them know you understand their feelings, whatever those are. We have a therapist here for the next few weeks. He's here for everyone—teachers, students, staff, everyone. Don't hesitate to talk to him. He's helped many people cope with tragedies like this one."

I search the group for Keely and spot her with Sally. When our eyes meet, she quickly looks at Pam.

"I contemplated having an assembly today, but I think we should all get comfortable in our classrooms. Do whatever you need to do to make your kids feel safe. You know I don't approve of movies as lesson plans, but I think I'll make an exception this week." She smiles. "On a sad note, there are quite a few kids who aren't ready to come back to school. I understand that. When they are ready, I'll let you know." Pam searches the crowd. "Keely?"

"Yes?" I hear her sweet voice from the back of the crowd.

"Callie will be attending school near her aunt's in the near future. Will you gather up her things for me? I'll take them to her this afternoon."

Keely clears her throat. "Sure. Of course." Her voice is broken, husky.

"Now, let's go get ready for our kiddos, my brave friends."

I look at the group again and see many are in tears. This is nerve-racking for them. When the group has thinned, I approach Keely and her friends. "Ready?"

"Yep," Michael says first.

Keely nods.

"I'll follow you."

They move slowly, taking their time getting to the door. When we cross the threshold, it's eerily quiet. No one is saying a word as they walk to their classrooms and workstations. Keely's group is no exception. We take the long way, arriving at Julia's room first. They all hug and watch her enter her classroom. Next is Sally's room. Same thing. Hugs all around. Even I get one this time.

"Thanks, Nick," she whispers in my ear.

Kimberly's room is next. I note new glass in Becca's classroom door, but there is no sign of the crime committed here a week ago. "Have a great day, guys."

Michael hugs Keely for several minutes. Before he walks into his room, he reaches out his hand to shake mine. "Thanks, Nick."

"No problem."

Keely moves to her door. Peering inside the small glass window, she sighs. "This is it."

I reach around her and pull her door open. "Let me check your room really quick."

"Okay."

She stands back as I enter the room, flipping on the lights as I go. I smile to myself, seeing how she's got her classroom set up. It's colorful, whimsical, fun. Just like her. I wish I'd had a teacher like Keely when I was younger. I would have probably enjoyed school a whole lot more than I did.

When I give the all clear, I move back to the door pushing it open for her. "You're good, Keely."

"Thanks, Nick." Keely seems so, I don't know, solemn.

Reaching out, I touch her upper arm. "It's going to be okay."

"I know." She looks up at me, her blue eyes watery. "I'm just emotional."

"Understandable."

"And..."

"And?"

Shaking her head, she adds, "Nothing. Never mind." Setting her bag on the desk, she pulls her chair out. Before sitting down, she smiles at me. "Thanks, Nick."

"Anytime, Keely." Anytime.

CHAPTER THIRTY-ONE

KEELY

THIRTEEN DAYS. That's how long we've been back in school. It took a good week for things to go back to normal—or to our new normal, I guess I'd call it. It's also how long it's been since I've seen Nick. Nearly two weeks since I've talked to him. Over two weeks since I touched him, smelled his delicious scent. And longer still since he told me he was done with me. Well, okay, he didn't say he was *done* with me but pretty much. He's done until I do right by him. I snort out loud and I hear a bunch of *shhs* coming from nearby shrubbery.

"Will you guys shut up?"

Ugh, that's from Sadie's asshole boyfriend, Andrew. *I hate that guy.*

"Sorry," I hiss. Not sorry if it's Andrew who's bitching.

If you're wondering why I'm in a bunch of shrubs, well, I'll tell you. My entire family, except Agatha, is hiding in the woods up at Lake Powell because her boyfriend, Ian, is going to propose to her at "their spot."

We've been hunkered down here for thirty minutes waiting for them to arrive. Hell, why do I have to be quiet? They aren't even here yet.

Just then, we hear a car approach.

I hear giggling that I know is coming from Lainie. God, I hope Keeton's not doing something to her in the bushes. Gross.

When I hear the car doors close, I decide to sit down on the ground and wait. I think I'm holding my breath now. My family remains silent in the hopes we'll be able to hear them. I crane my neck forward, but they're pretty far away. All I can do is watch. I know Agatha well enough to read her facial cues and gestures. Right now her hands are on her hips. She's in bossy mode.

"What's she saying?" I whisper hiss to someone closer to the action.

"She wants to know what the hell they're doing up here this late."

I snicker and reach out my hand to get hold of Violet's. She's behind me, slightly, and to my right.

"Now what?" I hiss again.

"Jesus, shut the fuck up."

Fucking Andrew Winchester. *I hate that guy.*

Lainie does us all a solid and narrates the action since she's closest. "Ian just gave her his sweater."

We all watch as Ian wraps Aggie up tight in his cardigan. She quickly wraps herself up into the warmth, then slides her hands in the pockets to keep warm. I'm holding my breath again, because this part was my idea. I told him to let her discover the ring. I know. I'm a genius.

I can't see Aggie's face from here, but I can hear her sniffling. "Is she crying?" I whisper to Violet, who is nearest to me.

"I think so."

"Goddammit. If you ruin this, I'll be fucking pissed. The game is on, and I'd rather be home doing that than here watching this bullshit."

"Andrew!" Sadie finally says something. "Be nice."

Be nice? Jesus. What is he? Twelve? Why she puts up with that tool, I'll never know.

OMG. "Is he on one knee?" I want to cry. Seriously. I feel wetness on my face, so I know it's happening. "Vi?" I squeak. Reaching out, I grab her hand. "I want that." I whisper it only loud enough for her to hear.

"I want that for you too, Keels."

I look up at my twin. "I want that for you too."

She stares down at me. Her eyes are intense. "I don't hate cops."

I blink up at her. Is she saying what I think she's saying?

"Especially one who saved my baby sister."

Oh, shit-dogs. "How?"

Violet rolls her eyes. "You think I'm an idiot, don't you?"

"No. But, who told you?"

"Everyone." She chuckles softly. "Literally everyone. But especially Michael."

The two of them are thick as thieves. Of course he'd blab to her.

"You sure?"

Violet laughs. "Yes. I'm sure."

Standing up fast, I get up on my tiptoes and hug my sister. "I love him, Vi."

"Good."

"I think he loves me too." Although I can't be sure.

"Of course, he does. How could he not? You're the bee's knees."

I find myself vibrating with laughter in my sister's arms.

Hers are wrapped tightly around me. "Yeah? Well, you're the cat's pajamas."

"Will you two shush up?" Lainie chastises us this time, so we do. I'm too busy smiling to say anything anyway. Plus, since we shut the hell up, we get to hear the end of the proposal.

I creep closer to the action. I finally hear Agatha say something. "That was, hands down, the most romantic proposal I've ever heard. The fact that it was for me, directed at me, makes me want to pinch myself. I wish you'd recorded it."

"We did!" Sadie yells from somewhere behind me.

Agatha looks down at Ian. "You invited my family? To our proposal?"

"I did, but they aren't allowed to come out from hiding until you've said yes. So, the ball's in your court. Do you want to drink the champagne I brought, or do you want to punish them for loving you almost as much as I do?"

"Oh, Ian." Agatha wraps her arms around Ian.

We can't hear what they're whispering to each other, so we wait until Ian announces, "She said yes!"

"Hallelujah," I mutter. It took her long enough. Now that we're all allowed to move out of the forest, we join the now-engaged pair for champagne and a gorgeous view of Lake Powell, one of my mom's favorite places in the entire world. Now it's one of mine, and not just because Aggie got engaged up here. No, this is the spot I discovered I can't love my twin any more than I do right now and that the minute I get back to town, I'm going to get my man.

CHAPTER THIRTY-TWO

Nick

I HAVEN'T SEEN Keely for two weeks. Well, thirteen days, if I'm being accurate. So, when I'm awoken by a knock on my front door in the middle of the night, I'm shocked to see her standing there. That's an understatement, to be sure. But damn, she looks beautiful. Sort of disheveled, like she's been hiking in the woods. I mean, I think there's even a twig in her hair. I want to reach out to see, but I'd better not. Without saying a word, Keely holds out a bottle of champagne.

"What's that for?"

"My sister Agatha just got engaged about an hour ago."

"Oh. Okay. Congratulations." I guess.

"I know. Ian's great." Keely is smiling at me shyly.

"Are you okay? Everything good at school?" I know it is. I've been checking in with Pam daily.

"Good. Kids are resilient. There are still three of mine, not counting Callie, who haven't returned to school. I don't think they'll be back. Some of the parents have opted to homeschool." She shrugs. "I get it."

I do too.

"But damn, homeschooled kids." She shivers visibly, then giggles. "They just don't get as socialized as the others, but they're alive, so I guess there's that."

I still haven't invited her inside my home. She's not a vampire, so I shouldn't be nervous about extending the offer. "Would you like to come in?"

"Sure."

What the hell is going on? I hope she's not here to play me. I meant what I said back at her place the day of the funeral. Keely hands me the bottle as soon as she's inside. "Do you want some?" I ask, holding up the bottle.

"Nah. Well, if you want some, I'll have a glass, but I'm good."

I don't want a drink, but I may need one after this—whatever this is. "I'll put this in the fridge." It'll give me a chance to regroup. "Make yourself comfortable."

When I return, Keely's sitting on the sofa. Not quite in the middle but close. She pats the seat next to her, but I pretend I don't see her doing that and sit in the chair across from her. The woman is my kryptonite. I could smell her scent as she passed me at the door, and my dick came alive. I don't need that right now. My wrist is sore as it is.

"So...," I ask hesitantly. "How are you?" WTF? I sound like a complete amateur.

"Great." She's smiling brightly. "I talked to Violet tonight."

"Oh? About?"

"Us."

"Us?"

"You and me." Keely is smiling. Her dimple's made an appearance.

"What did you say?"

"I told her I wanted what Aggie had."

"You want to get married?" Me too.

"Someday, but no, what I meant was I want that kind of relationship. Love." Keely looks into my eyes. "She told me she wanted that for me too and that she didn't hate cops. Especially one who saved me."

I look back at her, not quite understanding where this is going. "Good. I'm glad she doesn't hate cops."

"No." Keely laughs. "She was trying to tell me that she knew about you and me."

"How?"

"She said she heard it from everyone, but I'm pretty sure Michael blabbed. They're friends too."

Okay. Good to know. Still confused, I wait for the rest of the story.

"I told her you wanted to investigate Kyle." Keely's eyes start to get misty. "She said..." Keely's getting emotional. "Nick."

I start to go to her, but she shakes me off.

"She said she was tired of being sc-scared."

That's it, I'm going to her. I move around the coffee table to sit next to her. Placing my hand on her leg, I rub her knee gently so she can finish.

"I didn't realize she was scared, Nick. Almost six years later, she's still scared."

"It's not uncommon, Keely."

"I know. I, um, I just hate it for her."

"I know."

As Keely calms down, I can't help wondering why she's really here. Is it just because she wants me to look into Violet's assault? I've got to know. "Why are you here, Keely?"

"Oh," she says looking dejected. "I..."

"What?"

"I wanted to invite you to dinner."

"Dinner?"

"Tomorrow."

"Keely. I told you."

"At my dad's."

"At your dad's?

"I want you to meet my family."

Halle-fucking-lujah! "Yeah?"

"Yeah." Keely's smiling from ear to ear.

I stand up slowly. Leaning down, I cage Keely in with my arms. My voice is deeper than normal when I ask her, "You're sure?"

"Positive."

Without another word, I scoop her up, my hands beneath her ass as I walk her around the sofa and down the hall— straight to my bedroom. To *our* bed.

"No going back after this."

"No going back."

"Although..."

I stop in my tracks. I look down at her, ignoring the fact that my dick feels like it'll break in half if I don't get inside my girl.

"Can we take this thing slow?"

"Yes." I don't want to rush her down the aisle if she's not ready.

"I'm not ready to announce it to the world."

I arch my brow.

"Soon. Okay?"

"Soon." I'm not about to kick her out of my bed because she wants to postpone the rollout of our relationship. I get it. Sort of.

I set her on the edge of my bed and slowly undress her. I lean down and pull the small vine with a leaf out of her hair. "You in the woods, babe?"

"Yes. We had to hide until Ian was done proposing and Aggie said yes."

"Where was that?" I reach down and pull her sweatshirt from her body, then quickly unhook her bra.

"Lake Powell. It was so romantic, Nick." Keely says wistfully.

"Romantic, huh?"

"Yes." She stands up, pushing down her leggings and little panties.

I lose my tee and shorts too. Moving up onto the bed, Keely starts to roll over so she's on her hands and knees. "Not tonight, Keely. I want to see your face when I make you mine. For real. For good."

"Oh?" she says, sounding surprised. "I want to see you too."

She scoots back onto the bed, opening her legs so I can move between them. I feel her legs wrap around my hips, her feet dig into my ass, and her fingers slide up my shoulders, nails lightly scraping up to my neck. Her fingers move into my hair at the same moment I bring her pink nipple to my lips. I run my tongue over her breast once, twice, three times with the flat of my tongue, then I take her into my mouth, suckling her.

"Nick." She arches her back. Keely's nails drag across my scalp. "Nick. Now, I want you inside."

I shift until I'm at her entrance. I slide myself through her slit, making sure she's ready. Pushing inside, I move up and kiss her. Her mouth opens for me, and our tongues tangle. Chills cover my body, the hair all over me standing on end. I press all the way in and pause. I stop kissing just so I can look at her while we're joined. "You're mine, Keely May Palmer. All mine."

"Yes." She pants, wiggling around beneath me.

"Tell me you're mine."

"I'm yours. You're mine." She kisses my lips softly. "I love you, Nick."

"Fuck." I pull out and press in so slowly. "I love you too, Keely. Love at first sight."

I begin to move when she says, "Wait." She laughs. "You fell in love with me, then gave me a ticket?"

Oh, shit. I forgot about that. "Maybe?"

"Asshole." Keely shoves my shoulder, but not hard enough to knock me off.

I pump back inside her, deep inside her. "Sorry?"

"Forgiven." She moans. "Fuck. You feel perfect inside me."

"You feel perfect around me."

I'm close, so I reach down and run two fingers around her clit, pinching her lightly. I feel her tighten around me, and I come too soon. I can't help it. She said she loved me. I'm having dinner with her family.

I wrap her up in my arms and pull her to me. Kissing her forehead, I pull the throw from the end of my bed up and around us. "You make me so fucking happy, Keely."

"You make me happy too, Nick. I feel like I'm home."

Home. That's perfect. "Home."

CHAPTER THIRTY-THREE

KEELY

"EVERYONE, this is Nick. Nick, this is everyone."

Nick smiles at my entire family, standing at the entrance of my dad's house. There are so many packed in there that we can't actually step inside.

"Hi," Nick says with a small wave.

"Move, kids. Let me meet the man who saved my baby girl's life."

"He's her *boyfriend*, Dad," Sadie says, rolling her eyes.

"I know. Not only that, but he's my new best friend because he saved my baby girl. Now move." Dad chuckles as the Palmer family disperses back into his house.

Holding his hand out my dad introduces himself. "Rob Palmer."

Nick shakes. "Sir. Nick Martelli. Nice to meet you."

"Rob. Call me Rob, son."

Oh, shit. Dad broke out "son." That's it. He's in.

"Should we go inside?" I smile awkwardly at both men.

"You go ahead, Kiki. Let me talk to Nick here for a second." Kiki. My mom called me Kiki sometimes.

"Okay."

I step in and walk straight to the kitchen, to the fridge that houses the beer. Pulling out a bottle of some import Dad likes, I use the bottle opener mounted to the cupboard to pop it open.

"Is Dad 'talking' to him?" Lainie asks, using air quotes.

"He is."

"No worries. He's been dying to meet him since the..."

"Shooting."

"Yeah, that. He's wanted to thank him."

I take another long swig of beer. Damn, I'm nervous. "I've never brought a guy home to Dad."

"I know." Lainie throws her arm over my shoulder. "That's why we know he's your person."

My person. I never thought I'd get to say that. My mom called Dad that. It's why she gave up some of her dreams. She met my dad and those all changed. Dad was her dream. I feel myself tearing up at the thought, but I'm able to hold it back thanks to––beer. I take another long drink.

"Hm." I kiss Lainie's cheek. "I think he is."

"Think?"

"Know." I laugh. "I know. Okay? Geesh."

"Keeton likes him."

"A cop?" Don't motorcycle dudes hate cops?

"Not necessarily. Besides, Nick's not an asshole cop."

No. He's not.

When Nick finally steps into the kitchen, Lainie runs off while I offer him a beer. "Nah. I'm driving."

I shrug. "More for me." Then I cackle. Nerves. Sue me.

After that, things just sort of fall into place. Sure, the two beers helped, but mostly it was the fact that Nick rolled with it.

It takes a special man, a strong man, to be able to withstand the Palmer Inquisition.

So, while Dad grilled steaks, Keeton made some delicious kind of baked potato with seasoning salt, butter, and bacon, and Ian made the salad. And the Palmer girls interrogated Nick. I'd like to tell you that I felt sorry for him, but I didn't. He's a grown-ass man. If he can't handle the lil' ol' Palmer sisters, well, then... okay, just kidding. I was there to protect him from too many invasive questions, but no worries. My girls had my back *and his*.

I half expected Violet to bow out of the questioning, but she had a few good ones for him—none of which had a thing to do with the police force. No, hers related to knowing how to handle someone as high maintenance as me. I laughed my ass off at that.

But Violet was serious. "Keely. You know you can be quite abrasive and bossy."

"Yeah? And?"

"And I hope Nick knows what he's getting into."

"He does." Nick answered that one. "I love that about her. I'll just have to stay on my toes."

"Love? You *love* that about her?" Another one of Violet's.

"Love. Yes." Turning to me, he smiles. then looks at my sisters. "I love Keely."

Short and sweet. My man knows how to shut them down.

"Keely?" Agatha asks, beaming, her new ring glittering in the lamplight.

"What?"

"Do you love Nick?"

"My God, you guys are nosey as fuck. Yes." I laugh. "I love Nick Martelli."

∼

"WELL, THAT WENT BETTER THAN EXPECTED."

"You expected it to go badly?" Nick asks with one brow arched.

"Badly? Well, I think the words I had rolling around were crash-n-burn." I laugh. "No. I knew you'd be a hit."

We drive in silence for a few minutes. Only a few, because I have to know. "What'd my dad say to you?"

Nick looks over at me, giving me a sweet smile. "That he loves you dearly. That he doesn't know what he'd do without you. That he'll always be grateful I was at the school."

"Oh." I feel tears gather. "He's a great dad," I squeak. "He was our rock. Still is."

"I gathered that. That's why I told him I hope he's my dad too, someday."

That's it. Put a fork in me. I'm done. I start crying. and I can't help it. "Nick," I blubber. "That's so sweet. I bet he loved that."

"I wasn't trying to be sweet. I meant it."

"I kn-know. My dad is the most awesome pops in the world."

"He'll be a wonderful grandfather."

"Nick." I whine and sob, and then slap his arm. "You're killing me here."

"Sorry." But his face did not read "sorry." It read "victory."

CHAPTER THIRTY-FOUR

KEELY

Five Months Later

"FLUCKITY-FLUCK-FLUCK," I moan the minute I see flashing lights in my rearview mirror. I must have been too busy singing along to my favorite song to pay attention to my driving, because I just noticed those lights behind me.

"I know it's not Nick." Because he's out of town doing his school training seminar. The requests for Nick's training program have gone through the roof. He's been traveling at least once per week all over Arizona since the local ABC News station did a story on him and his training. I miss him when he's gone, but he's doing important work, so I can spare him now and then if it makes teachers and administrators feel safer, more empowered. Not to mention saving kids.

I'm pulled from thoughts of my brave man when I see movement in my side mirror. "If this guy knows Nick, I may be able to talk my way out of this." There's no way they'd give another cop's girlfriend a ticket. Right?

From the side mirror, I watch a man clad in black police gear, stride to the driver side of my car. I lose sight of him for a second, so I roll down my window and spot him in my side mirror.

"License, registration, and proof of insurance please, ma'am."

My mouth is agape. What the hell is going on?

"Ma'am. I haven't got all day."

I scan up the black uniform, noting how perfectly pressed the thing looks, up to the badge on his meaty pectoral.

MARTELLI

"Nick?" I squeak. "What are you doing?" Why is he here?

He's supposed to be down in Flagstaff.

Please don't tell me he'd give his girl a ticket. Oh, hell, of course he would.

"Ma'am? Did you hear what I said? License, registration, and proof of insurance. Now."

Damn, he sure is demanding. Wait! Maybe this is some kind of kinky role-playing thing that Nick likes but has never mentioned. Like ever. No way he's going to give me a ticket. I'll just play along.

"I'm sorry, Officer, but what did I do?" I flutter my eyelashes and ever so subtly push my shoulders back so my chest sticks out just a tiny bit.

With a very heavy sigh, he pulls his glasses off his face, revealing golden brown irises and long dark lashes. "Excessive speed and your taillight is out. Again."

Why is he complaining about that? He said he fixed it. *Men.*

Wait! This must be his idea of role-playing. "My taillight is out?" I put my finger on my lip and give him my best pout. "You'd better spank me."

"Excuse me?"

Wow, Nick actually looks pissed. Note to self. Spanking is out. Damn it.

Doing my best to look unassuming and cute, I place my palm on my chest like a southern belle fanning herself, and I flutter my lashes once again. In a breathy Marilyn Monroe kind of voice, I say, "Officer. I didn't mean anything."

I watch his eyes roll.

"Ma'am. I'm only going to ask one more time. License, registration, and proof of insurance."

Flustered now, I grab my purse from the seat beside me. What the hell is going on? Everything was fine last night. We had dinner like usual, watched a little television, and fucked like rabbits.

"Today, ma'am."

I give him a little dirty look but say sweetly, "Oh, sure. Let me find them."

Then, I hear his voice rumble even louder as he asks me, "Do you know how fast you were going?"

I turn my head toward him and smile. Bam, there it is, my dimple. "Um, the speed limit?" See, how adorable was that response? I sounded a little dumb but still cute.

"I don't have all day, ma'am."

"Right. I'm getting it. Hold your stupid horses."

"Excuse me?"

"I said, hold your stupid horses, geesh." What's going on? Damn it. Nick isn't playing. I swear, he's really going to give me a ticket.

"Step. Out. Of. The. Car. Was that clear enough for you?"

"Well, yeah, but you don't have to be a jerk." Forget I ever considered him good-looking. Or nice. Or my boyfriend. Now he's Officer Jerk-Ass.

I quickly unbuckle my seat belt and exit my car.

"Please move to the back of the car. Place your hands on the trunk." I know why he has me move to the back of the car instead of on the side nearest the road. He told me about Melissa, his partner in Phoenix. According to his friends down there, she's improving every day.

"Yes, Officer Bossypants."

Silence.

"Is this really necessary?"

"Please stop talking, ma'am."

He begins the pat down at my shoulders, and his hands move down my sides slowly. Really, really slowly. He's taking an extra-long time as his big, warm hands slide down the sides of my breasts. Actually, his palms move below my breasts enough that I feel him bump them. I'm about to moan, I mean protest, when his hands slide down the front of me like he's going for gold, but he quickly moves them back to my hips, down to my ankles, then back up to my ass.

"Turn around, ma'am."

God, I hate when he calls me ma'am. Turning around quickly, I'm ready to look up and glare at the ass-face, but he's not there. No. He's down—on one knee.

"You asshole," I say, laughing, then crying, the minute I see the little box in front of me. "Nick?" I say, all weepy and shit.

"Keely May Palmer. You're a spitfire and the love of my life. I need you to be my wife and the mother of my kids like I need air to breathe." He pauses, looking up at me. "Marry me?"

"Serious?"

Nick chuckles. "Serious. Say yes."

"Yes," I screech, throwing my arms around him. "I love you so much." I'm kissing his neck, his cheek, his nose, when I notice clapping. Lots of clapping. Turning slowly, I see we've got an audience. They're all standing in the same parking lot where Nick gave me my warning ticket so many months ago.

My family, of course, and my best friends, and a bunch of cops.

I turn back to look down at Nick, still on his knee. "Nick, you planned all this?"

"I did. Was it romantic enough for you, baby girl?"

"It was sort of mean-spirited at first, but I get where you were going. It's how we met."

"It was."

Nick holds up the little box that looks like a small wooden cube. I gaze at the ring, blinking many times. "It's perfect."

"Just like you."

I snort and give him an eye roll for that one. "I'm not perfect."

"You are for me. Perfect for me."

I admire the yellow gold band with a square-cut yellow diamond. "I've never seen anything like it."

"One of the first things I noticed about you was your hair. It reminded me of the sun. That's why I picked this one. It hasn't been sized, so if you don't like it, we can—"

"I love it, Nick." So much. I slip it from the box and hand it to him. Holding out my left hand, I let him slide it on. "It fits. It's a little too big but not much."

I wrap my arms around him again and kiss his neck. "I love you so much. You could have put a ring from a bubble gum machine on me and I'd love it."

"Well, damn. I could have saved money if I'd known that." He chuckles. "I'm serious. If you want to choose—"

"Shh. I love it. It came from you. You thought about me when you picked it. There's no other ring that could compare."

He kisses me gently. "Let's go show our family and friends."

Our. He said "our" family and friends.

"Yes, let's." I turn and smile at our family and friends, raising my hand to wave.

Nick adds, "We're meeting at Murphy's to celebrate tonight."

I get up on my tiptoes, wrapping my arms around his neck. "Yay. Hot wings!"

"You're more excited about the hot wings than you are about the engagement party your sisters arranged, aren't you?" Nick deadpans.

"No." I kiss his cheek. "They're just a bonus."

Before hopping back into my car, I turn to my family and wave again. A family that is expanding every minute, and I'm not just talking about babies that'll be coming soon. No, I'm talking about literally expanding. Take Lainie, for example. She and Keeton tied the knot last month in a big, fancy church deal. Keeton insisted on giving Lainie the wedding she never got with Lewis. Then we've got three more happening soon. Cortland and Polly's nuptials are in a couple of weeks; Aggie and Ian set a date of March 6 of next year. One year to the day after she was fired from her job. It was also the day she met Ian.

That's romantic as shit. I wonder when Nick and I'll get married. Maybe a year from the day he gave me my speeding ticket? Hmm, no. If it's going to be the anniversary of anything, it'll need to be a good memory. *Stupid tickets.*

I look over at my twin. She's beaming at me. I know she's happy about Nick and me. She never shuts up about it. But I think the real reason she's so happy for me is because I'm pretty sure she's met someone too. Someone we all like, someone we know will take care of her heart. At least I hope so. God, I hope she falls in love. If she can find a way to open up herself to the idea, I think he's got a shot. I'll do what I can to help that along, but it's ultimately Violet's decision.

I look to my left and see my dad. He's smiling from ear to ear at me, but there's something else going on too. *Oh, Daddy...* the most amazing man I've known. I quickly slide into my car and drive over to the parking lot where everyone has been watching. Pulling up behind my dad's car, I throw it into park and jump out, running into his arms. Now that I'm close enough, I can tell he's been crying. "Daddy?"

"I'm fine, Kiki; I'm so happy for you both. He's a good man. I couldn't have chosen anyone better for you."

"I know," I whisper in his ear. "Do you think Mom would have liked him?"

"She'd have adored him. He saved her baby's life. How could she not?"

My eyes fill with tears, and one slides down my cheek. "Thanks, Daddy."

"Now," he puts me back onto my feet, "Murphy's is on me tonight. All the hot wings you can eat, Kiki."

I smile big. "I can't wait."

As I turn to approach my sisters, I see Michael and my little gang from school. We meet halfway, each one hugging me and checking out the ring. "It's gorgeous. Why a yellow diamond, though?" asks Sally.

"Because it reminded him of my hair. It was the first thing he noticed about me." I'm smiling so hard my cheeks sort of hurt.

"Aw, that's romantic," adds Julia.

"That's the first thing he noticed about you? It wasn't your big mouth?" says smartass Michael.

Punching Michael in the arm, hard, I laugh. "That was second, numb-nuts."

At that moment, I'm surrounded by the rest of my family, all talking at once. They all love the ring and the way he proposed. When I feel big, warm hands wrap around my waist, I lean back into him. I feel so safe. Not only that; he makes me happy. But do you want to know the best part? We're friends. Best friends. And isn't that what they always say? You should marry your friend, not your lover. But here's the kicker—I've got the best of both worlds.

God, I'm a lucky bitch.

Being Kennedy's

Quirky Girl

For a complete list of Kayt's books, visit:

Kayt's Website: www.kaytmiller.com

ACKNOWLEDGMENTS

Thank you to Olivia at Hot Tree Editing for editing this book from start to finish.

And an extra special thank you to Becky at Hot Tree Promotions for your advice, expertise, and your positivity.

And for my beta readers.
Thank you so much for your time and feedback!

ABOUT THE AUTHOR

Kayt grew up in the midwest surrounded by a loving family which included three brothers, one sister, and parents who always fostered her creative side.

Kayt wrote her first book when she couldn't find a story about a certain type of a woman and a specific kind of man. She called it *Game Changer* and it couldn't have been a more appropriate title. It changed her life in many ways.

Her goal, as a writer, is to write stories that relate to all of us, to make readers laugh and maybe cry sometimes. Kayt hopes her readers can escape into a fantasy, one that's actually possible. Sure, some of the stories are dubbed "Insta-love" but that's okay. She fell in love with her husband pretty damn fast and with her daughter the second I saw her. So, it's a thing, I swear.

 facebook.com/authorkaytmiller

 twitter.com/kaytmiller1

 instagram.com/kaytmiller1

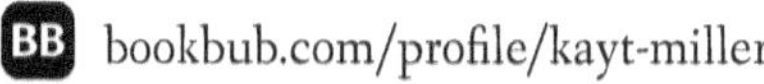 bookbub.com/profile/kayt-miller

The Palmer Sisters Cover Designs
by
Colleen Galligan
galligancolleen@gmail.com

Colleen,
Thank you for all of your hard work
and creativity on the new covers!
I love them! KM

THANK YOU!

Thank you so much for reading Keely and Nick's story! When I start a story, it begins with an outline, notes, and lots of crazy thoughts running through my head. When I actually start writing, the characters take over, leading me through the story like they're holding my hand—guiding me. The process is exciting and cathartic. With that said, I hope you enjoy the story.

If you did, please go to my website, www.kaytmiller.com, and join my newsletter so you can be the first to know what's coming up next. And...

And remember...Please, leave a review!

Thank you!

Chapter 1: *Violet*

"Hey, Violet."

I look up from my hiding spot in a shady corner of Keeton and Lainie's lower patio to see Nick Martelli approach.

Here we go.

Stepping closer, he points to the lounge chair next to me. "May I?"

"Of course." I know what's coming. I just didn't expect us to talk about it at my sister's rehearsal dinner. At least we're secluded back here; no one will be able to hear us.

"I've got news," Nick says as he sits on the side of the chair so he's facing me.

"News?" I'm not looking forward to this conversation at all. I've been dreading it, actually. We've had exactly two talks about Kyle Maines: Two excruciatingly uncomfortable and painful conversations. In the first one, back in May, Nick told me what he knew about Kyle, things that both surprised and frustrated me. First of all, he lives in Sedona. A city only about

150 miles straight south of Page. Not a surprise since I've seen him twice here in town. One of those times, the first time I've seen him since *it* happened, he approached me at Murphy's Pub.

Kyle is what you'd call well-connected. His mom is Frances Abernathy, the Lieutenant Governor. Of *Arizona*. At the time *it* happened, she was the Pima County District Attorney. To be specific, she was the D.A. of Tucson. So, even if the Tucson police had done their job, nothing would have happened to Kyle anyway. She'd never have prosecuted her own son. It's no wonder the cops did what they did.

At our second 'talk,' I gave Nick a copy of my original police report. What good it'll do for him; I have no idea. I'm sure the Tucson P.D. have it too.

Nick sighs. "So, here's where I'm at on this, Violet."

A sigh isn't good. I lean forward in anticipating bad news.

"You know I've been working on this off duty, right?"

I nod. I knew he was doing his best to keep the promise he made to my twin, Keely. She didn't want me to have to deal with any of this again, and I don't either.

"And you know I've only been talking to people I can trust."

I nod again. He's been doing everything he can to keep things quiet. "I know. Thank you."

He arches his brow. "I'm not going to be able to keep doing it."

"What? You're done investigating?" I'm not sure how I feel about that. I mean, I hate Kyle Maines. I'd love to see him rot in jail, but the idea of it just going away is okay too.

"No. I won't be able to keep it quiet."

Oh. "Oh? Why not?"

"You weren't the only one."

"Oh." I say softly. I knew that was probably the case. The

guy knew what he was doing that night. It felt like it was all choreographed or something.

"In every city he's lived in there have been complaints filed, but..."

"No charges?"

Nick nods slowly. "No charges."

"Because of his mom?"

Nick nods, wincing. I can see why. The Arizona Police have dropped the ball.

"How many others?"

"Keep in mind this is just speculation—educated speculation. My contact in Tucson says the cop in charge when you went to school in Tucson is gone. That's why they were able to dig into the archival records for other possible victims. That cop is now in Sedona."

I gasp. "Oh, my God. How is that possible? He moves wherever Kyle lives or something?"

"It seems that way, but we haven't looked into that yet. That's why I'm telling you this thing has to expand."

"So, you think that cop has been working to keep Kyle out of jail."

Nick nods while saying, "Yeah, I think so. "

"Then there are more." It's not a question, of course there are. He was at the University of Southeast Arizona for four years and president of that fraternity for three of those. "Where else has he lived besides Sedona and Tucson?"

"He grew up in Scottsdale," Nick says. Scottsdale is a very wealthy city just outside of Phoenix. "His parents still have a home there. I've only been able to learn of one incident there when he was in high school."

Poor girl. I look up at Nick. "What about recently? In Sedona?"

"Nothing so far. But he's a predator and I'm guessing a serial rapist. He's not going to stop since there's no one to stop him."

"Until now."

"Until now." Nick gives me a little smile. "There's no doubt in my mind if he hasn't done it yet, he will. It's been his permanent residence for almost a year. It's only a matter of time."

I nod, hoping we can stop talking about Kyle soon. I'm starting to feel anxious. I do my best to keep Kyle from my thoughts. I guess that's not going to be possible now.

"Luckily, my friend in Tucson was able to do a little research on the sly." Reaching into the back pocket of his dress pants, Nick pulls out a folded piece of paper. "Your original police report."

I take it from him and quickly scan the report. "This isn't..."

"I know. It was doctored sometime after you left the station."

"Why?"

"Read it." Nick pauses. "Please."

I don't want to read it, but I will. Sighing, I start at the top. Everything related to my name, address, and my vital statistics are correct. But when you get down to the part where it summarizes the incident, it's different. Where mine goes into disgustingly great detail about what Kyle did to me, this one was much shorter, changed to:

Synopsis: *The alleged victim in this case, Violet Leigh Palmer, age 19, reported she was sexually assaulted by possible suspect Kyle Joshua Maines at Omega Alpha Pi fraternity located on the University of Southeast Arizona campus.*

Narrative: *Miss Palmer alleged that she met Kyle*

Maines at the party. She stated that he was concerned at the level of her intoxication.

I snort at the words. "'Concerned with the level of my intoxication'? That's a lie."

"Keep reading."

She alleges Kyle took her by the hand and led her upstairs to a bedroom that she assumed was Kyle Maines's room. There, he told her to lie down on the bed to rest but Maines claimed she didn't want to be alone, so Kyle climbed into bed with her...

Shaking my head, I look up at Nick. "I can't...that's not what happened. This is nothing like my report."

"I know."

"Can't you just show them mine?"

"It's easy to recreate documents these days." He shrugs.

"So, just like the rape, it's my word against the Tucson police?"

He nods, but says, "If you were the only victim, I'd say yes, but since we know of others..."

"You can get their police reports?"

"We hope so. That's why we need to open this up. I can't keep it a secret anymore. As a matter of fact, we may need to go public. As in, notifying the press."

I lay my head back onto my lounge chair. I knew this would happen. Looking over at him, I ask, "Do you think his mother knows?"

Nick arches his brow. "Yeah." He nods. "She's got to know."

"How could she let him...?" I mean, she's a woman. "Why would you stand by a man who raped multiple women, even if he *is* your son?"

"I have no idea, Violet." Nick reaches his hand out and touches the top of my wrist, patting my hand gently. "So," he clears his throat. "You need to prepare yourself."

I look up suddenly and my eyes meet Nick's. "Huh?" *What's he talking about?*

"I can't sit back and risk him hurting another woman, Violet. I need to make this an official investigation. I need to get the captain up to speed. As it is, he's not going to be happy that I've gone rogue on all this."

I stare at his face and blink like I've got something in my eye. I think I do. Tears. But I won't let those fall tonight. Not when we're all so happy about Lainie and Keeton.

Nick leans forward whispering, "Shh. It's going to be okay, Violet. I promise you. I'll keep you safe."

How can he say that? It's going to get out. Everyone will know. I won't be able to keep this secret anymore.

"Violet." He pauses. "It's time you talked to your family."

I shake my head slowly, but I know he's right. It's time they all found out why I'm such a freak of nature. Why I'm the weird one in my family, why I turned inward almost six years ago and have been working all that time to bring myself out of it. When it happened, I dropped out of college. I couldn't stay there. I literally packed my bags the day the police told me they didn't believe me, and never looked back. I lived with my dad for a year, working part-time jobs here and there. Since then, I've gone back to school. I've been making progress. I hate this. It's going to hurt the people I love the most. I scan the crowd for my dad, and I spot him near the pool talking to Keeton's ex-wife, Deb. He's smiling and I watch as he throws his head back, laughing at something she said. There's no one who deserves to smile and laugh more than my father. Finally, after all these years, he's happy and this news, this drama, is going to kill him.

"Violet. It's time," Nick whispers.

I know. Turning back to Nick I say, "Give me until after Keeton and Lainie get back from their honeymoon." No way am I telling them tonight or tomorrow, their wedding day. "Can you do that?"

"A week then?" he asks.

I nod. "A week."